Sunshine

a novel based on a true story

LEE   SILBER

ALSO BY LEE SILBER

The Homeless Hero
Runaway Best Seller
Summer Stories
Show And Tell Organizing
No Brown M&Ms
The Ripple Effect
Creative Careers
Bored Games
The Wild Idea Club
Rock To Riches
Chicken Soup For The Beach Lover's Soul (Contributor)
Organizing From The Right Side Of The Brain
Money Management For The Creative Person
Self-Promotion For The Creative Person
Career Management For The Creative Person
Time Management For The Creative Person
Aim First
Notes, Quotes & Advice
Successful San Diegans
Dating in San Diego

Sunshine

a novel based on a true story

L E E   S I L B E R

SUNSHINE

Lee Silber

Published by Deep Impact Publishing
822 Redondo Court
San Diego CA 92109

To buy copies of this book in bulk, inquire about a presentation based on this information, or get a free copy of the companion guide featuring more of Sunshine's advice not included in the book, please contact the author at:

www.leesilber.com, 858-735-4533, leesilber@leesilber.com

Cover Design: Lee Silber
Interior Design: Lee Silber

First Printing September 2016

This is a work of fiction. All the names, characters, and places are either invented or used fictitiously. The exceptions are the real people or places Sunshine specifically wanted included in this book.

Retail Price: $11.00

This book is dedicated to a bright light in an otherwise dark world, my friend, Sunshine Blake.

—LEE SILBER

To the universe and all the opportunities it provided me to explore everything life had to offer.

—SUNSHINE BLAKE

"Life is infinitely stranger than anything which the mind of man can invent."

—SHERLOCK HOLMES

ACKNOWLEDGMENTS

A big thank-you to K. Shawn Gibson and Ruth Klampert for their support. The folks at Soleluna deserve credit for keeping Sunshine and me well fed (and caffeinated) while we sat and talked for hours on end. I want to acknowledge all of the editors who helped shape this book, including: Steve Benbow, Pam Chana, Diana Chase, Judy Feeley, Ellen Goodwin, Deborah Gunn, Georgann Koenig, Andrea Redd, Annette Silber, Mary Valerio, and Louise Wills. My good friend and writing partner Andrew Chapman was helpful once again with this book. Finally, I've been blessed to have had Sunshine on my shoulder for over 20 years—she was a constant source of light, warmth, and hope. She lived her life as an inspiration to others and changed my life for the better.   **—LEE**

To the two brightest lights in my life, my sons Shawn and Kirit. To all the instructors and people who have shown me the lessons I needed to learn and shaped my philosophies and my life. If I hadn't met them, I wouldn't be the person I am.   **—SUNSHINE**

CONTENTS

INTRODUCTION

This book is based on a real person, Barbara Blake—better known as Sunshine—who lived the most amazing life. She loved, she laughed, she cried, she succeeded, and she failed; however, no matter what was happening in her life, she had that special ability to make you feel better about yours.

Nobody would ever guess Sunshine made and lost a fortune, was widowed four times, lost her home and all of her possessions in a fire, or that she was abused and abandoned by her parents. Instead, people found her fascinating because she was fascinated with them. Her mission was to live a full life and inspire others to do the same. This book shares her story and continues her legacy, but it almost didn't happen.

I originally met Sunshine in 1994 at a publishing forum I hosted at a Barnes and Noble in Del Mar, California. Well over a hundred people attended the event, but only one made a lasting impression on me. Sunshine stayed after everyone left and we sat on a bench in the back of the store and she told me all about the book she was going to write—but never did.

After always looking for the next big adventure in her life, Sunshine was finally forced to slow down and reflect on her past when she was diagnosed with terminal cancer in 2009. In a race against time, Sunshine and I met nearly every Wednesday for coffee and chatted about everything she'd done and seen in her extraordinary life— the good, the bad, and the ugly.

This is the story of a woman who had every reason to be negative and instead found ways to be positive no matter what happened to her—and a lot happened to her. Sunshine saw the bright side of life even in the darkest of times. She simply couldn't understand why people used their past as an excuse for their unhappiness in the present. Sunshine is gone, but her message of hope and happiness lives on.

I want to share Sunshine's story of perseverance and pass on her message—the universe provides you with everything you need to succeed and be happy. There is no excuse to not go after what you want and enjoy the journey along the way. Sunshine teaches us to live by our own rules, follow our hearts, and take chances on the things we believe in. Her outlook on life is worth exploring and could possibly change yours for the better.

So read this book to be inspired, entertained,

thrilled, informed, humored, moved, and motivated. This is the kind of book everyone wants to read whether they like a good story, need a pick-me-up, enjoy a thriller and mystery, or find it fascinating to learn about the life and times of an extraordinary person and her many adventures.

Through the Years

1956

THE UNWANTED GIRL

EIGHTEEN YEARS OLD

Sunshine had been through a lot of storms in her young life—both literally and figuratively—but the fierceness of the weather on a summer evening in Biloxi was downright frightening. She was accustomed to winter storms where everyone hunkered down to wait out the snow in the north, but this was her first severe storm down south, and her first hurricane—and it was going to be a doozy.

She was holed up in a small motel room with three other teenage girls. The four decided to watch television to distract themselves from the potential disaster of the developing storm just outside their flimsy door. But the gale force winds must have blown the antenna from the roof because the stations were static instead of the black-and-white picture they had hoped for. The resourceful girls wheeled the bulky television across the room to use as a wedge to prevent the front door from being blown wide open.

The wind blew the rain sideways against the windows of the small room and sounded like machine-gun fire. The immediacy of the storm had all four on edge. The sporadic thunderclaps in the distance made the girls' hair stand up and reminded them the worst was still to come. The howl from the wind was so loud it seemed as if a train was passing by at full speed. The clanking of the rigging on the boats just a block away meant the raging ocean was right around the corner.

The two-story motel seemed safe since it was made of brick and the front faced away from the nearby harbor. The girls were given a corner room on the second floor just in case there was a storm surge and the first floor flooded—which had happened to the motel in the past. The motel manager checked on them earlier in the afternoon and assured them they would be fine, but the truth was, none of them wanted to be there in the first place.

Since the girls were traveling as part of a group selling magazine subscriptions throughout the South, they couldn't just hop in a car and outrun the storm since they didn't have a car, or control over their time. Instead, their boss (and probably his boss at the Union Circulation Company in Atlanta) decided it was better to stay put—

but only after the girls met their sales quota for the day. Sunshine was new to the group and didn't dare speak up, but the others weren't happy with how their day had played out and the danger they were in.

Since Sunshine was the newbie, the other more experienced girls insisted she be the one to go outside and see what was happening—and buy them each a Coca-Cola from the vending machine next to the lobby. At ten cents a pop, Sunshine was reluctant to spend her hard-earned cash on soda, but agreed to go for the good of the group.

Dressed only in peddle-pusher pants, a short-sleeved blouse, sneakers, and a kerchief to hold back her hair, Sunshine forced open the door and was blasted by the wind and rain. She had to hold onto the railing to make her way along the balcony and down the stairs, shielding her eyes as she went.

On her way to the front office she glanced up for a second to look around and noticed the parking lot was completely empty. She feared she and the girls had been abandoned by their boss, which was exactly what had happened. The white Pontiac station wagon they arrived in was gone, as was the motel manager's beat-up old Ford that she saw him loading up earlier in the afternoon.

Scared and angry, Sunshine put her head down

and rounded the corner to where the lobby was located. The wind was steadily increasing and Sunshine watched in horror as a large portion of the motel's signage was ripped off and carried away by the storm. The lobby was locked and it looked like nobody was inside. Frightened and frustrated, Sunshine yanked hard on the door, but nothing happened. Something off to her side and behind her caught her attention and she jumped out of the way just as the soda machine was blown over and into the glass door—shattering it.

Sunshine hesitated before stepping over the glass and into the lobby. Always one to do the right thing, she decided that if she made it through the storm, anything she took would be returned or paid for when it was all over. She looked around the lobby and began to fill an empty trash can with whatever supplies she could find. She rushed back to the room—banging on the door until the girls heard her and let her in.

"You're drenched," Dottie yelled, and forced the door shut.

Bobbi handed Sunshine a towel and asked, "What the heck is going on out there?"

Drying herself off, Sunshine smiled and said, "Well, I have some good news and I have some bad news. Which do you want first?"

Kat, who was sitting on the floor with her knees to her chest asked, "What's the bad news?"

"Okay, first of all, we're all alone here at the motel."

"Whaddya mean, all alone?" Kat wanted to know.

"I mean, everyone left, and left us here alone. Even the motel manager is gone."

Kat pulled her knees even tighter to her chest while the other two girls paced around the room. "I can't believe the crew leader left us here all alone. I'm gonna kill him when I see him," Dottie said with conviction.

"You said you had some good news," Bobbi wondered.

"Yes, I was able to get into the lobby and bring back a bunch of supplies," Sunshine said, pointing to the trash can on the floor filled to the brim with goodies.

The girls pounced on it and pulled out several bottles of Coca-Cola, a pack of Lucky Strikes, a Zippo lighter, a Philco portable radio, two flashlights, an assortment of batteries, candles, Oreo cookies, a box of Ritz crackers, a jar of Planter's Peanuts, and a bottle opener. The girls were thrilled with the haul and almost forgot about the storm.

Kat was the one to ask first, "What's it like outside?"

"Obviously, it's really windy and the rain is coming down pretty hard—and sideways. There's nobody on the

5

street, and the front door to the lobby just shattered, but other than that, it's not as bad as it sounds."

Kat wasn't convinced. "Is the water going to cross the street and flood the first floor of the motel?"

"Even if it does, so what? We're on the second floor," Sunshine pointed out in as positive a tone as she could muster.

Kat just rocked back and forth on the floor.

"Let me change out of these wet clothes and I'll tell you more about what I saw outside," Sunshine said. She handed Kat her current issue of Life magazine she used as a sample to sell subscriptions. "Why don't you read this?"

When Sunshine came back from the bathroom in clean, dry clothes, Dottie, Bobbi, and Kat were all sitting on one of the beds smoking cigarettes, listening to Elvis on the portable radio, and poring over Life magazine. "Look, here she is again in a Revlon ad."

"Who are you talking about?" Sunshine asked, feeling a little left out.

"Suzy Parker, of course," Kat replied, clearly feeling better and forgetting about her fears—for now. The sounds of the storm were still loud, but now they were familiar and not nearly as terrifying. The radio also helped to drown out the wind and rain to some degree.

"Who?" Sunshine asked.

"The model on the cover," Dottie said, turning the magazine over so Sunshine could see. "She leads the most interesting and glamorous life."

"Her real name isn't Suzy, you know, it's Cecilia," Kat proudly pointed out.

"Is Sunshine your real name?" Bobbi asked.

"No, but it's what I've been called for as long as I can remember."

"What is your real name?" Bobbi wanted to know.

"Barbara, but nobody calls me that," Sunshine said, watching Kat turn the pages of the magazine as she looked over her shoulder.

"Not even your mother?" Kat asked, looking up at Sunshine.

"My mother," Sunshine said, and blew out a long breath of air. "My mother doesn't call me anything, because I don't talk to her anymore."

"You don't talk to your own mother? Really?" Dottie asked. "I call my mom every day from the road, and it ain't cheap."

"It's a long story," Sunshine sighed.

"Hey, we've got time. Why don't you tell us about your mom?" Bobbi asked.

The girls all got comfortable and turned to face Sunshine, eager to hear about her life.

"It's not a happy story," Sunshine said while twirling a strand of her long hair.

"So what. If you can't tell your life story to a group of girls hunkered down together in an abandoned motel with a hurricane heading their way, then when can you tell it? Am I right?" Kat asked.

"I guess, but it's really embarrassing."

"How about this? After you tell us about your life, we'll each take turns telling you about ours. Deal?" Kay said.

"Deal," Sunshine said.

Just as Sunshine was about to tell the tale of her childhood, the power went out. At first everyone panicked, but after lighting the candles Sunshine had borrowed from the front desk, and using the flashlights as spotlights, the girls gathered around to hear Sunshine speak about her life.

"Where should I begin?" Sunshine asked.

Dottie quickly answered sarcastically, "How about at the beginning?"

"Right. Well, I was born in Easton, Pennsylvania on January 11, 1938. I'm pretty sure I wasn't a planned pregnancy, and I think my parents wanted to put me up for adoption, but they got married instead. My father was a truck driver who delivered Dixie cups and my mother worked in a factory baking cakes. I didn't really know my parents because they were never home."

"You mean they put you up for adoption after all?" Kat asked.

"No, worse, they both abandoned me. My father was never around, and then my mother ran away and left me with my grandfather, but he didn't want me either," Sunshine could barely get the words out as she choked up.

"That's so sad," Kat said.

Through tears Sunshine said, "It's a horrible feeling when nobody wants you—not even your own parents, grandparents, or any of your relatives."

"So where did you live?" Dottie asked.

"Nobody knew what to do with me, so I went to live with foster families, usually for a month or two at a time. So I never really had a home."

Even though the room was only lit by candles, Sunshine could see all the girls had tears in their eyes. "It wasn't all bad, I guess. I learned how to deal with different kinds of people and get along with just about anybody. So that's good. I know it made me stronger and more self-sufficient," Sunshine added, meaning every word of her appraisal of where she'd been and where she was going.

"What about school?" Bobbi wanted to know.

"I was never at the same school for a whole year, so I was always the new kid—an outsider. I remember in the first grade I entered a costume contest. I'm part Ukrainian, so I dressed up in an authentic dancing costume that was brought over from the old country. I practiced and practiced and I did a whole routine, but I lost to a girl in a plain white dress because her father was the President of the PTA. It wasn't fair, but I learned a lesson from that experience. Right is right and wrong is wrong, but life isn't fair. People with money, power, and influence can change the rules. So, I decided I would always do the right and ethical thing to set an example for others to follow."

None of the girls in the room came from wealthy families, so they could relate, but nobody came from a place of poverty like Sunshine did. Dottie asked Sunshine, "Did any of the foster families you lived with have money?"

"Nope. Not one. I got used to being poor, I guess. The one thing that saved me was books. I always loved to read, and the library was like my second home."

"Were you a good student?" Kat asked.

"I thought so, but in the third grade I was sent to yet

another school in the middle of the year. At the start of the year, the teacher had divided all the students into two groups, the smart kids on one side of the classroom and the dumb ones on the other. She even named the groups. The fast learners were called the Rabbits and the slow kids were called the Turtles. Since I was new, the teacher didn't know what to do with me, so I was put in a group all by myself. It was horrible. I didn't feel like I belonged anywhere, and the teacher made me look silly. The kids teased me mercilessly."

"Oh my God, that's terrible," Kat said.

"At first I cried myself to sleep every night and when that didn't help, I decided to make the best of the situation. I had to toughen up or I wouldn't make it through the year. So I named my group of one, 'Sunshine and the Smarty Pants,' and then studied extra hard to get into the Rabbit group."

"Did you ever get into the Rabbit group?" Dottie asked.

"I did, and I was proud of that, but I also learned to love being on my own, too. I realized at a young age that if it is to be, it's up to me—and not depend on others to make things happen for me. Instead I have to make them happen for myself.

I transferred to another school later that same year

and had the best teacher ever, Ms. Hulsizer. I think she took pity on me. She told me to find the positive in everything and focus on it instead of dwelling on the negative—and there were a lot of negatives. She also told me to have confidence in myself and to be myself, no matter what others say or think."

"Did you make friends at school?" Bobbi asked.

"I wasn't the most popular kid in class, that's for sure. I think everyone thought I was weird because they didn't really know me. On my ninth birthday, I asked my foster mom if I could have a party and invite some of the kids from my class to come over. My foster mom, Mrs. Rivera, didn't want to pay for the party or hold it at the boarding house, but I begged her and she came around. Looking back, it wasn't the perfect place for a kid's party because Mrs. Rivera would take in anyone who would pay rent, and most of the people who lived there were either truck drivers or ex-cons just out of jail.

"The State paid her to take care of me, but to cover the cost of the party, Mrs. Rivera reached out to my mother. My mother said she would bring a birthday cake from the bakery where she worked and would help decorate the house. I was over the moon. A lot of my classmates came to the party, which was a pleasant surprise, but my mom never showed up. I kept telling the kids from my class that she would be there and we would all have cake, but my mom missed the party, which ruined everything. The kids called me a liar, took back their meager presents, and they all left. It was awful. Just awful."

"So your mom never showed up?" Kat asked.

"No, she eventually showed up, but she was drunk and it was long after everyone had left. She rang the bell and I was so happy to see her even though she wrecked my party. She had a squishy cake in her hand that looked like it was half eaten, and no present. I begged my mom to take me with her, but her boyfriend was waiting in the car and he kept honking the horn and yelling at her to hurry up so they could go—without me, of course. My mom shoved the cake into my arms and walked off. The cake got all over my dress and Mrs. Rivera beat me for making a mess."

The girls stared at her dumbfounded by what they'd heard. Bobbi asked, "What did your dad do when you told him about how you were being treated?"

"My dad never came to see me at the boarding house. I only remember meeting him once when I was four. He took me on a wild motorcycle ride that scared me half to death. Wait, there was one other time I saw my dad. It was Father's Day and I was visiting with a cousin who told me my father lived nearby. She showed me where he lived, but before I went to the door, I went back to my cousin's house to make him a Father's Day card. Later that day I went back alone and rang the doorbell. After a few minutes the door opened and I said, 'Happy Father's Day' and I tried to open the screen door to hand the card to him and give him a big hug. He stared at me like I was from Mars and held the screen door shut so I couldn't get in and said, 'What the hell are you doing here?' Then he slammed the front door in my face.

Sunshine couldn't hold back her emotions any longer and began to bawl from retelling the tale about the encounter with her father. After she composed herself she said, "My father is the way he is. I can't blame him for how he is, or even get mad. I can't change him or the situation. It is what it is. It made me realize that it doesn't matter what happens to you, it's how you deal with it. I decided to not play the blame game. My teacher, Ms. Hulsizer, was right, I had to focus on the positives. I can't choose who my parents are, but I can choose to be happy no matter what the circumstances—and that's what I've done. I find solace in learning because knowledge gives me strength, and I find joy in reading because it provides me with an escape."

"Did you ever try to see your mother again?" Kay asked.

"If I wanted to see my mom, I had to go to a bar. She was a shuffleboard champion, you know, the kind you play with small metal disks on a wood table with sand on it so they would slide easier. Every time I saw my mom she was drunk and mean, so after a while, I decided to just stay away."

"Now I know why you don't talk to your mom every day like I do," Dottie said. "I guess that also explains why you're always reading and your little yellow suitcase is so heavy. You have more books than clothes in there."

"I've always lugged a lot of books around. One time my teacher asked me what I was reading and when I told him I was reading three books at once by Jung, Nietzsche, and Adler, he asked me why I wasn't reading comic books like normal kids. I told him I wasn't normal, so he sent me to the library to find some light reading. Can you believe that?"

"Your teacher wanted you to read comic books?" Kat asked.

"Who are the authors you said again?" Dottie asked.

"I think it's over your head, Dottie," Bobbi chimed in.

"Hey, there's no need to be mean," Kat replied.

Sunshine jumped in, "I was always questioning what life is all about, and those authors had the answers. Don't you ever wonder what the meaning of life is?"

Sunshine asked, realizing right away that was the wrong question to ask. The three girls just looked at her and said nothing.

Mercifully, Kat took a stab at the question. "To get married and have kids, I guess. What else is there?"

"To not die in a hurricane in a dingy motel?" Dottie added.

Sunshine decided to tell them about her interpretation of what living a full life meant. "I also want to get married, and I don't want to die in a storm, but I also don't want to die with any regrets. When my teacher told me to go to the library to look for some light reading, I did. I found an article in a magazine that changed my life. I guess that's why they call it *Life* magazine," Sunshine said, trying to lighten the mood, but it didn't work.

"So it was *Life* magazine then?" Dottie asked, not realizing how silly her question was.

"Yup. There was an article about a centenarian," Sunshine said, and quickly realized she should clarify what that meant, so she added, "You know, a person who lives to be a hundred or older. Anyway, in the article the writer asked the man, 'Do you have any regrets?' He said, 'Well, I don't have a lot of regrets about the things I've done, but I have a lot of regrets about the things I didn't do.' That's when I started thinking about all the things I want to do before I die."

"What if we all die today?" Kat wanted to know.

"Well, of the things I want to do, I've only done a few of them, so that's why we're gonna ride out the storm and I'll add 'survive a hurricane' to my list and then check it off," Sunshine said, pleased with her idea.

"I have no idea of what I want to do with my life," Bobbi announced, and then added, "I do know what I don't want to do. I don't want to sell magazines any more. This is my last jump. After this, I'm going back to Chicago. I just want to live a normal life from now on."

Sunshine added, "You know how I said I was always wondering about what the meaning of life is? To me the word 'life' is only one letter away from 'live,' so I want to live my life to the fullest. Normal is fine, but I want an abnormal life—I want to see the world and learn new things. Since I was a straight A student, my teacher didn't care if I missed class, so I spent the rest of the day in the library making a list of the 187 things I wanted to do before I die, or turn one hundred years old, whichever comes first."

"Was magazine sales on the list?" Bobbi asked.

"Not exactly, but the ad you all answered was probably the same as the one I saw. It asked, 'Are you free to travel?' When I was in the library that day and I made my list, travel was my number one goal, so I signed up to sell magazines."

"Yeah, I saw the same ad," Kat said. "But it didn't say anything about being ditched in Biloxi during a hurricane."

"I didn't have that many options anyway, so this seemed like a good idea, and all in all, it is."

"For you, Sunshine, it's working. In the two years I've been doing this I've never seen anyone else skip going out on the town at the end of the day like you do so you can sell more subscriptions. In a way, you're kinda making us all look bad by going way over quota."

"Yeah," Bobbie said.

"Well, I don't have a choice. I have to make this work because I don't have anything to fall back on. In school I didn't learn to type because I didn't want to be a secretary. When I worked at a restaurant in Atlantic City, I acted like I couldn't carry plates, so they made me a hostess instead. Which was much better, by the way. With my good grades, I could have gotten a scholarship to go to college, but I wanted to make money right away, so here I am."

DEAR DIARY *When I was telling my story to the girls it made me realize something that has served me well over the years, no* *matter how bad you think your childhood was, mine was worse, but I've never used it as an excuse—and other than that fateful day, I never really talked about it. I've met so many people who say they ended up as a drug user, prostitute, criminal, or were abused because of their childhood. I say hogwash. My parents didn't want me, I grew up in foster homes (some of them worse than others), and I was always poor, but I made it through and became a better person because of it.*

I believe you are in charge of your life. Bad things happen to good people all the time. You can choose to be a victim, or you can choose to be a victor. You can't let what happened to you in the past determine what happens to you in the future—unless it makes you better, wiser, and stronger. I am going to live my life with no restrictions and no regrets. I want to live a full life and leave nothing on the table. It doesn't matter where I came from, what matters most is where I am going, and I am going places.

1960

GIRLS ONLY IN
THE VIRGIN ISLANDS

TWENTY-TWO YEARS OLD

"This never gets old," Sunshine said to a new member of the magazine crew seated next to her in The Goose, a large seaplane that took passengers island-hopping in the Caribbean.

The plane banked and lined up for its final approach in the waters just off Beef Island on the eastern tip of Tortola. "It's beautiful," Sally said, looking out of her small window on the starboard side of the plane. "Look at all the different shades of blue in the water. Are those little white dots sailboats?"

Sunshine had to speak loudly since the propellers were quite noisy. "Yup, and we'll be on one tomorrow when we start selling. See the hotel over there at the base of the green mountain?" Sunshine asked, as she pointed to a large resort located right on a beach. "That's where we're staying. You did bring a bathing suit, right?"

"Oh yeah. I just splurged on a brand new Carol Brent two-piece."

Sunshine patted the small bulge in her Capri pants and said, "I'll have to switch to a one-piece, since I'm pregnant," She announced.

"Did you say you're pregnant?" Sally yelled over the roar of the engines.

Before Sunshine could respond the seaplane hit the choppy water, bounced, and bounced again before settling in as the plane became a boat. It was still noisy, but the two women could talk in more normal voices now.

"I can't believe it. You're going to be a mom."

"I know, I'm only 22 years old, but I'm trying to look at it as my next big adventure."

The plane taxied on the water toward a dock where the passengers would disembark. "Are you married?"

Sunshine showed her the ring on her finger and said, "We just got married in Mexico, and then I went to Texas for a few days before I came back down here. That's why I was able to meet you and fly down on the same plane. The rest of the girls are waiting to greet you at the hotel."

"Your husband isn't here?"

"Oh no, he has his own crew in the States."

"He sells magazines, too?"

"Mmm-hmm, that's how we met. David's a hot shot in the South. In fact, he's the number one salesman in the company, so he's got his own crew and territory. I fly up and we meet from time to time to, you know, do it. I can't believe I got pregnant. When I found out, I decided we should get married, but still live separate lives," Sunshine said while the plane was being secured to the dock.

"Why don't you just join his crew?"

"And give up all this?" Sunshine asked as the plane's door opened and a warm breeze wafted in tinged with the fragrances of the tropics.

Later, Sunshine introduced Sally to the other girls in the crew as they lounged poolside at the hotel, when one of them said, "Welcome to the Virgin Islands, but some of us," she said, nodding at Sunshine, "aren't quite virgins." The four of them all laughed.

"Is it always this warm here?" Sally asked.

"Yup. It's 85 degrees year round," one of the girls replied.

"Is it safe?" Sally asked.

"It's safer here in the BVI than the AVI," Sunshine answered.

23

"What's the AVI?" Sally wondered.

"The American Virgin Islands. As you know, we're in the British Virgin Islands right now. The AVI is to the north of us. The reason it's such a great place to sell subscriptions is everyone speaks English and they use our currency down here. In addition, we're the only ones here doing what we do so people are thrilled to get their hands on anything new they can read."

"Do they pay us up front?" Sally asked.

"They do. I call in the sales to the office every Friday and we send them the cash and checks in the mail. It's also the only way we get the latest news and updates."

"So when do we start?" Sally asked.

"Tomorrow. Here, look at this map and I'll show you where we'll be over the next few days." Sunshine pointed out the exotic sounding places on the map including Frenchman's Cay, Virgin Gorda, and Jost Van Dyke. "Tonight, we're going into Road Town for some rum and fun, so you should work on your tan today because tomorrow we're on the clock and your training begins."

"Aye, aye, Captain," Sally said and slipped her hip new sunglasses back down over her eyes while stretching out on the lounge chair overlooking the ocean below. With the warmth of the sun on her face, the intoxicating sea air in her lungs, and a long day of travel behind, Sally quickly fell asleep by the pool.

After a day in the sun, the girls got ready in their adjoining rooms and headed down to the lobby to wait for a cab to take them into town. Since everything worked on "island time," it could be a while, so Sunshine and the crew regaled Sally with stories of their Friday nights on the town, telling her about dancing with the locals (and tourists) to the sounds of island music well into the wee hours of the morning. How they barely survived the crazy cab rides through the steep, narrow, and winding mountains and why they drive on the wrong side of the road.

Sunshine shared a few of her favorite places to eat and what to watch out for. She made sure to warn Sally about the rum drinks that can make you do wild and crazy things like dance on top of tables and jump in the water in just your skivvies—all things Sunshine could personally attest to.

"Sunshine, show Sally your photos," one of the girls said. "Sunshine never goes anywhere without her camera and she takes the best pictures. Look."

Sunshine pulled a pocket-sized photo album out of her purse and handed it to Sally as they all gathered behind her to point out where the pictures were taken and what was happening in each one. Sally thumbed through the first few of Sunshine and the girls posing next to an old fort, lounging on hammocks strung between trees, and having drinks at bars on the beach. Suddenly she stopped at one photo and stared. "Where is this? Is this a pool?"

"No. It's a place called The Baths, and the water is so clear you can see the shadow of your boat on the bottom at fifty feet. Whenever we pass by it while crossing the channel, we make the boat driver stop so we can jump in. Incredible, huh? The water is so blue it looks fake. Plus it's warm. There's some great places to snorkel there, too," Sunshine said.

"Where is this?" Sally wanted to know while pointing to a picture of the girls posed in their bathing suits on top of a rock overlooking the ocean."

"That's a place called The Dogs. We had to swim in and climb up the cliffs for that picture. The boat driver took the picture and then pretended to leave us stranded there. Remember that?"

All the girls nodded and added their own stories about their amazing time in the Caribbean. Sunshine pointed to one picture in particular and said, "There's a lot of sailboats anchored in the sheltered coves, so we rented a small dinghy one day and went boat to boat taking orders. It wasn't that successful because boaters don't have a permanent address for their subscriptions, but boy was that fun.

A lot of times they invited us aboard for drinks and to chat about what was happening stateside—which we didn't know much about because we're based here.

There's a few bars on the beach where you can only get there by dinghy so we would beach our boat, mix with the regulars, and have them buy us drinks. We didn't sell many magazines, but we sure got sloshed," Sunshine said with a smile, and all the girls giggled.

Sally, now the newest crew member, flipped through page after page of pictures of the sales crew of having the time of their lives. Then she stopped and stared at a group shot and asked, "There's a girl in most of these pictures who isn't here. Who is she?"

"Doris."

"She's beautiful."

"I know. Which is why when she met a rich guy with a big yacht anchored off Spanish Town, she quit to sail around the islands with him. Can't blame her. That's why you're here, Sally. We're short one girl."

"Shoot. I almost forgot," Sunshine said, and suddenly left heading for the elevator. "I haven't called the office yet with your sales from the week. Since I was gone and got married, it kinda slipped my mind. I'll be right back."

When Sunshine returned she couldn't speak. "Sunshine, what's wrong?" one of the girls asked.

"I… I… I'm a widow."

"You're a what? You just got married, how can you be a widow?"

"David was killed in a car crash on Monday and the funeral was on Wednesday. Nobody could get hold of me because I've been traveling, so they were waiting for me to call in to tell me what happened."

"Are you okay?" Sally asked.

"I think I'm in shock. I can't believe David is dead."

"What can we do?" The girls asked as they gathered around Sunshine for a group hug.

"Nothing. It's not like he was the love of my life. He was just fun to be with…" Her voice trailed off.

"The baby!" Sally blurted out.

"It's okay. I've always been independent, I'll raise the baby on my own. I'm not so sure David would have been the best parent, anyway. He wasn't exactly thrilled when he found out he was going to be a father. It'll all work out, it always does."

"Do you want us to help you pack?"

"Why? I'm not going back."

"You're not?"

"Why would I? There's nothing to go back to.

There's something else I didn't tell you. David wasn't alone when he crashed. There was a girl with him. She's dead."

"That's horrible. What happened?"

"I don't know, but they said there is no way anyone could survive the crash, even though they never found David's body in the wreckage."

The girls talked about this new revelation while Sunshine sat down and thought about what she should do next.

As it turned out, what she would decide to do next would surprise everyone, herself included. Sunshine wanted to leave the warmth of the Caribbean and head north—way north—for a bold new adventure in Alaska.

"If you don't mind me asking, what brings you to Alaska," Ozzy, the pilot said into the headset microphone.

"It's a long story, but the company I work for suggested I give it a try, and I needed a change of scenery, so I said yes," Sunshine replied, while looking out of the window of the tiny two-seat pontoon plane she rented to take her to some of the hard-to-reach places in Alaska. "Plus, it's beautiful up here."

"You say that now because it's summer. Wait until winter comes and see how you like it."

"I won't be here that long," she said, and then asked him why he was here.

"Well, I first came to Alaska to become a commercial fisherman, which I did, but then I fell in love with flying and the rest is history, as they say," Ozzy said, while keeping his attention focused on flying the small plane.

There was a long silence and then the handsome pilot spoke, "You know, usually I fly fisherman, firefighters, and oil people around, but a few months ago John Wayne was here making a movie called, *North to Alaska*. I never flew The Duke around, but I did take the director around to scout locations. I think his name was Henry Hathaway. Do you like movies?"

"I'm a reader, which is why selling magazines is something I like to do. I'm hoping there are enough people here in Alaska who like to read like me."

"What magazines are the most popular?" Ozzy asked, trying to make small talk with Sunshine.

"My favorite is *Life* magazine, *Time* magazine would be second, *Look* and the *Saturday Evening Post* are also big sellers," Sunshine said.

"There must be easier ways to sell magazines than renting a plane to visit remote campsites," the pilot said.

"Yes, but it's a lot faster by plane."

"It's your money, but wouldn't a car or boat be

cheaper... and safer?"

"No, because cars can crash and boats sink," Sunshine said.

"I've got news for you, lady, sea planes can both crash and sink. Do you know how to swim?" Ozzy wanted to know.

"Not only can I swim, but I know how to parachute as well."

"Interesting. I don't know many women who can parachute. In fact, I can't think of one."

"When I was younger, I made a list of things I wanted to do in my life and parachuting was on it, so I did a half-day class in the morning and then I jumped out of a plane in the afternoon."

"I learned to jump when I was in the military," Ozzy stated and then said, "Hang on to your hat, we're almost there."

The plane banked to the right and Sunshine was able to get a good look at the water below. "How cold is that water?" she wanted to know.

"Oh, it's cold. But you don't have to worry because Sitka is straight ahead, and unless I screw up this landing, which I won't, you won't have to get wet."

The town of Sitka was a lot less developed than Anchorage, but it still looked like any small town in the lower forty-eight (as the rest of the United States were known to those living in Alaska). There was a hardware store, diner, movie theater, Post Office, and several bars. Sunshine headed for the diner to get something to eat and meet the locals.

It didn't take Sunshine long to hit it off with the waitress, who bought a subscription for herself and one for her mother, and then introduced her around telling the regulars she was new to town, pregnant, and needed their help. The good people of Sitka—and Juneau, Ketchikan, and the dozens of campsites Sunshine visited—all ordered magazines. The unusually long summer days (over 20 hours of usable daylight) made it possible for her to cover a lot of territory in one "day" and make enough money to save up and take some time off to have her baby—which she did in Texas.

DEAR DIARY *I tried to feel something for David when he died, but the truth was it was like losing a friend or an acquaintance instead of a husband. I wasn't really ready to get married or start a family—especially with him—and I now know he felt the same way about me because 16 years later while talking to his aunt I found out he didn't die in the car crash after all. His passenger died, but they never did find his body. He faked his* *own death and actually died years later of a heart attack.*

He didn't want to be with me and didn't want to raise his son—his loss. When Shawn was born it was such a blessing. Three months later I took him with me when I returned to the road to sell subscriptions. It turned out having a baby boy was the big adventure I thought it would be. I'm a big believer that everything happens for a reason, even if we don't know what the reason is at the time. If we have faith that everything will be okay—that we'll be okay—life can be a lot less stressful.

1962

A FLIP-FLOP LIFE ON THE EAST COAST

TWENTY-FOUR YEARS OLD

"You look like you just stepped out of Vogue magazine," Joe said to Sunshine when she entered the kitchen of the large New Jersey farmhouse they shared with a few other friends.

"I'm meeting a Realtor at my office. He's got someone interested in buying that fixer-upper I'm trying to flip," Sunshine said, and twirled around to show off her snazzy new pantsuit.

"Sure you don't want to go out and sell subscriptions with us today?"

"Nope. I'm doing just fine buying and selling real estate," Sunshine said while putting two slices of bread in the toaster.

"But you don't even have your real estate license."

"And it hasn't stopped me yet," Sunshine said over her shoulder while getting the butter from the fridge.

"You were making good money selling magazines, too, and with a lot less risk I might add."

"You're right. In the past two years I saved up $5,000 from my subscription sales, but I've saved up $10,000 from my real estate deals in just the past few months. How about that?"

"Huh. I should be charging you rent," Joe said.

"You are. I take care of the horses and I cook for you boys. Want some toast?" Sunshine asked when the toaster dinged and two burnt pieces of bread popped up, which she buttered anyway.

"No thanks. Oh, by the way, can you take the horse out for a while when you get done with your wheeling and dealing in town?"

"Be glad to," Sunshine said, munching on the burnt bread.

Sunshine's "real estate" office was about the size of a closet, with only enough room for a desk, two chairs, and a filing cabinet—but it was hers and she was proud of it. She chose to set up shop in Manville, a tiny town in north New Jersey, because it was less than an hour from New York, but it seemed like a world away. Manville was situated next to North Plainfield and just off Route 22, so sometimes Sunshine would just hop in her car and drive around the two towns looking for homes with "potential" that she could buy. Since she was conditioned to hearing "no" and being rejected her whole life, she had no trouble knocking on doors and asking people if they would be interested in selling if she saw a promising property.

Today, she had the top down and a bandanna wrapped around her hair as she drove her Corvair convertible down the country road that would take her to town. She got the car for far less than it was worth because the original owner felt the way it handled made it too dangerous for his wife to drive. Sunshine was more than happy to have such a slick car, even if it was a potential death trap—especially since she got it on the cheap. Sunshine parked on the street in front of the old brick building in the center of town and saw her morning appointment walking toward her.

"Hi, Bill. Right on time," Sunshine said while checking her watch.

"Same goes for you, Sunshine. Time is a valuable commodity and I don't like to waste it, so I'll get right to the point. If you'd be willing to take $12,000 from the buyer for your property, we have a deal," the Realtor said.

"That's more than the asking price," Sunshine said,

doing the math in her head and quickly realizing that after all the real estate transaction fees she would clear $2,000 for something she only owned for a month—and she would now have $17,000 to invest in her next project.

"I know. The buyer I represent is eager to tear down that dilapidated thing you call a house and build something beautiful in its place—near the creek. So is that a yes or a no to the offer, Sunshine?"

"How can I say no? You've got yourself a deal," and the two shook hands.

"Oh, and the buyer wants to pay cash," the Realtor said while pulling the paperwork from his briefcase.

"Even better," Sunshine said with a smile.

Sunshine was on such a high from her good fortune that instead of reviewing the papers needed to finalize the transaction, she jumped in her car and went searching for the next big thing. Most of Manville was flat, and ever since she was a child, she believed poor people lived in the low-lying parts of town while the rich people lived high up in the hills. So that's what she wanted now that she was successful, a house on a hill—and she found one fairly fast.

Sunshine drove up a dirt road that led to a radio tower so she could get a better look at the town below.

She figured she would start at the highest point and see what looked like a good piece of property below. She parked next to the base of the tower and looked around. In the distance she could see the house she was currently living in at the bottom of the hill. That gave her a good point of reference. Now all she needed to do was a little research to find out what was available for sale near here—the higher up the hill the better, because the view was spectacular.

The following day while closing the sale on her former piece of property Sunshine asked Bill if he knew anything about the land at the top of the hill with the radio tower.

"Oh, yes. That land belongs to Elsie McCray, and trust me, she's not selling anytime soon. We've all tried, but she's not the least bit interested. That land has been in her family for as long as I can remember and that's the way it will likely stay."

"Does she have any kids to pass it on to?" Sunshine wanted to know.

"Nope. She's all alone up there with her cats."

"Hmmmmm."

"Sunshine, I know what you're thinking. Be careful, she's armed and dangerous. Every time I've been up there to see her about something she's pointed a loaded shotgun at me."

Sunshine was lost in thought about how to strike up a conversation with the reclusive Elsie McCray and didn't hear the Realtor's warning.

"Sunshine, you want me to complete the paperwork and have it recorded?"

"Yes. Yes. That would be wonderful, Bill. Thank you."

Sunshine drove straight home, parked the car, ran to her room and changed into the worst pair of pants she could find to go with the worn out denim shirt she planned to wear on her ride to meet the eccentric Miss Elsie.

It took Sunshine a while to find the house on the hill since she was now on horseback and looking at it from a different perspective—but using the tower as a guide allowed her to find the land and eventually the vintage home. She slowed her horse to a trot as she rode by while the old lady on the porch glared at her but didn't say anything (even though there were "No Trespassing Signs" clearly posted all around the property).

Every day at lunchtime for the next week-and-a-half, Sunshine rode by the house on horseback. Sometimes Sunshine would wave and the old woman would nod just a little, but the shotgun still stayed on her lap as she rocked back and forth watching warily as Sunshine passed by. Then it finally happened. The old woman waved her over.

"That's a beautiful horse. Don't see many people riding up here," Elsie McCray said while rocking in the chair on her expansive porch.

"I'm so sorry. I know you have all these signs posted to stay away, but the view from up here is so wonderful I just couldn't help myself, and neither could Hot Rod here. He loves climbing the hill," Sunshine said, steadying the horse. "We live down at the bottom."

"You have my permission to ride by whenever you two want," the woman said, putting the shotgun down on the ground next to her.

"Thank you. My name is Sunshine. What's yours?"

"Elsie."

"Thanks again, Miss Elsie. Hot Rod and I will see you tomorrow," Sunshine said as she rode away with a big grin on her face.

Over the next few days Sunshine made it a point to ride by, wave, and say hello to the lonely old woman who now smiled and waved back. To get to know Elsie better, Sunshine decided to make lunch for the two of them and walk up the hill instead of riding by the following day.

"Hi, Elsie," Sunshine said while walking up to the

porch. "Have you had lunch yet?"

"I, uh, well, no."

"I made sandwiches. Want one?"

"Well, if it's not too much trouble."

"No trouble at all."

"Where's Hot Rod?"

"He's, um, I don't know how to say this, he's at a neighbor's house with a neighbor's horse. A female horse."

"Ohhhhh."

"Hot Rod is happy about it, but I couldn't ride him up here today, so I thought I would walk up for a change."

"I'm glad you did."

The two sat and ate in silence until Sunshine said, "Is all of this land yours?"

"Yup. My granddaddy bought the property and built this house in 1890. It's been in our family ever since and I've lived here my whole life."

"It's so peaceful and beautiful up here," Sunshine said.

"It was a lot nicer before I was forced to put in that monstrosity over there," Elsie said, nodding toward the radio tower behind her house."

"At least you don't have to look at it if you don't want to," Sunshine said, trying to keep the conversation light.

"I didn't really have a choice. I needed the rent money the company that owns the tower pays me to get rid of those darn Revenuers."

"Revenuers?"

"You know, the tax collectors. I hate 'em all. I know they want me to sell, but I'm not selling."

"Who wants you to sell?"

"Everyone. The Revenuers, the Realtors, my neighbors. I don't care how much they offer me, this is my home and I'm not leaving."

"I know how you feel. I wouldn't want to leave here, either," Sunshine said, an idea forming in her head. "There may be a way you can stay and get those Revenuers off your back. Let me do some research and tomorrow I'll stop by and see if the solution I have in mind makes sense."

"I'm not moving."

"If I'm right, you won't have to."

The next day Sunshine rode up the hill on Hot Rod to see Elsie and share the solution to both of their problems— Elsie needed money to pay off the back taxes she owed, but didn't want to sell her house and have to move. Sunshine wanted to buy land overlooking the town but didn't want to displace Elsie. So she worked out a way for them both to get what they needed and wanted.

"I think I have a way for you to keep your home and garden just the way it is and stick it to the Revenuers at the same time," Sunshine said.

"I'm listening."

"You spend all of your time out here on the porch taking in the view, right."

"I think you know the answer to that, Sunshine."

"You've got your garden over here to the left," Sunshine said pointing to the rows and rows of fruits, vegetables, and flowers thriving in the direct sunlight. "You have the rolling hills and the view of town in front of you, and the road to the right."

"Sunshine, I may be old, but I'm not blind. I know where everything is."

"Exactly. Everything you see and enjoy is in front of you, in front of the house."

"So?"

"Most of the land you own is behind you—and your house. What if you planted a row of large trees out back to hide the tower and sold off the rest of the land on the back forty?"

"I need the money from the tower, though. I'd keep that."

"Of course."

"What do you think I could get for that land?"

"I'm prepared to offer you $17,000 for it."

"You?"

"Yes, me. I want to be your neighbor. I love it up here."

"Sunshine, you're an angel."

"I don't know about that, but I do know the best deals are the ones where everyone wins."

"Except them darn Revenuers."

"Yes, except them."

Over the next few months, making sure the land deal went through was all Sunshine thought about, talked about, and worked on. Since it was a complicated transaction, and she wasn't a licensed Realtor, she needed help. She turned to her friend Bill, and cut him in on the deal in exchange for his assistance.

They decided to subdivide the property and sell off parcels to help pay for the home Sunshine was planning to build. Immediately they received offers for some of the other prime home sites—and sold the rest shortly after that. Money was flowing in and the only expenses they had were the few things they promised to do so Elsie would be happy on her side of the development. The rest of the money was put in the bank while they waited for the permits to begin building—except for Sunshine's sales commissions, which she kept for herself.

This was it. She had made it and she was going to enjoy it. During the winter of that year Sunshine escaped to Puerto Rico for a few days every other week to soak up the sun. Along with her big deal, Sunshine was now making money on other smaller real estate deals as well. She rented a condo by the beach in San Juan with a pool and other amenities—including a safe where she smartly stashed some of her earnings—which made it the perfect winter retreat… and tax haven.

From the very beginning Sunshine drew the ire of other Realtors in town who were furious that she was somehow able to do what they could not—get Elsie to sell. In a small town like this, some of the power players were also in the real estate industry, and they used their influence in local government to stall Sunshine's plans at every step. They even complained to the IRS and Federal Government that somehow, there was fraud being committed—which wasn't true. This led to all the money related to the deal being frozen while the IRS and other government agencies investigated—after they were pressured by the town's political heavyweights and their cronies. It wasn't long before Sunshine and her partner lost everything when they couldn't keep up with the mortgages since their assets were frozen. It was a devastating loss for Sunshine, but one she would bounce back from—as she had her whole life.

DEAR DIARY *I went down to Puerto Rico one last time—and I'll admit, I cried. A lot. I was so close to my dream. Then I realized, that was one heck of a ride, even if it didn't end the way I wanted it to. A year later I received a letter from the government stating that I was cleared of any wrongdoing—but it was too little too late. Most of the money I had stashed down in Puerto Rico I used up trying to keep the government from taking the land, but when I realized it was a losing battle I saved a little so I wouldn't be totally broke. But I lost a lot. The way I look at it, I started with nothing and I made thousands of dollars. If I did it once, I could do it again.*

1965

HER VERY OWN HERCULES

TWENTY-SEVEN YEARS OLD

Even though Sunshine had been living in Los Angeles for a time, she still had yet to really see the sights. One place she wanted to explore was the famous Venice Beach. She'd heard Jack LaLanne talk about the bodybuilders who worked out and showed off in "The Pen," a fenced in area with weights and workout equipment right on the beach.

What she wasn't quite prepared for was the spectacle it truly was, as bikini-clad women watched the weightlifters demonstrate their strength—and agility. As she walked up to "The Pen," she witnessed a man lifting up two girls, one on each arm. Another was doing push-ups with three large men on his back, and others were showing off their feats of strength with different acrobatic maneuvers.

LEE SILBER

"Why is he hanging upside down like that?" Sunshine asked a very muscular and handsome man who seemed to be the center of attention.

"Because he can," the man replied with a thick accent.

"Oh. I'd like to try that sometime."

"Why not now?"

"Uh, I'm wearing a mini skirt," Sunshine said as she did a quick curtsy.

"So you are. What's your name?" the muscular man asked while flexing.

"Barbara, but everyone calls me Sunshine."

"Nice to meet you, Sunshine. I'm Arnold."

"I like your accent Arnold, where are you from?" Sunshine said with a big smile.

"Austria," Arnold said while waving to a fellow bodybuilder who was leaving "The Pen."

"I'm going to Europe," Sunshine announced.

"Today?" the man asked while he flexed his chest muscles.

"No, someday. I have a list of things I want to do and places I want to see."

"It's good to have goals. My dream was always to move to the United States and compete for a title, and here I am."

"So you're a bodybuilder?" Sunshine said, lowering her sunglasses to get a better look.

"No, I'm the bodybuilder," Arnold said with a smile.

"I see. What about those guys over there?" Sunshine wanted to know.

"Come, I'll introduce you," Arnold said, easily lifting her over the low fence.

"Hey guys, come meet Sunshine. Sunshine, meet the guys." Several pumped-up and sweaty men in shorts shook her hand and said hello.

"The guy hanging upside down is Lou Degni, but now that he's a big movie star, people call him by his stage name, Mark Forest."

He did an upside down sit-up and pulled himself up before hopping off the bar and walking over. "You can call me Lou."

"You're a movie star? But you're not that tall. I mean... "

Arnold and the others laughed so hard they almost fell over, walking away to at least let Lou retain a shred of dignity.

"I'm so sorry. I don't know why I said that," Sunshine said, slowly backing away.

"It's okay, you'd be surprised how many actors are shorter than you think. But none of them are built like me," Lou said while flexing his muscles in a few different poses. "Plus, I can sing."

"You can sing? You. Really?" Sunshine asked, unable to hide her surprise.

"Okay, that's two insults in a row. I think you owe me an apology or I can take you to dinner and we'll call it even," Lou said.

"I'm sorry, I didn't mean it like that."

"So that's a no to dinner, too?"

"No, I mean, yes. Of course, I'll have dinner with you," Sunshine stammered.

"Good. It's a date then. I'll pick you up at seven tonight. Where do you live?" Lou asked.

"I'm staying with Jack LaLanne and his family. I help out with the business, watch the kids, and walk the dogs—mostly I walk the dogs."

"You're friends with Jack, that's good. That's real good. I like you already. Tell Jack that Lou Degni says hello. It was because of him, Joe Gold, and Vic Tanny, that Muscle Beach even exists. I haven't forgotten that."

Sunshine turned to say goodbye to Arnold and the other bodybuilders when Lou got down on one knee and began singing a perfect rendition of "My Girl" by the Temptations. Then some of the other bodybuilders gathered around and joined in on the chorus. Sunshine blushed while she walked away, turning back more than once as she left to head down the boardwalk.

Lou pulled up to the LaLanne home in his red sports car. It was a little too small for his large frame, but he loved it nonetheless. He parked in the circular driveway and made his way to the front door of the large house.

"Is Jack home?" Lou asked.

"I'm sorry, who are you?" Elaine, wife of the fitness guru, asked the stranger at her door.

"I'm Lou Degni, perhaps you've heard of me?"

"I can't say that I have."

"Like your husband, I'm a bodybuilder," Lou puffed out his chest just a little as he said it.

"I can see that," Elaine said.

"I'm also an actor. For my films, I go by my stage name, Mark Forest. I've been in over 13 movies."

"Anything I may have seen?"

"Well... *Goliath and the Dragon, Hercules Against the Barbarians...*"

"No, that's not my cup of tea, but I think it's good that you used bodybuilding as a springboard to success. Jack isn't here, but I'm sure he would have liked to meet you," Elaine started to close the oversized front door as she said it.

"I've always wanted to meet your husband. He inspired me to open my own gym in Long Island before I came to California and became an actor."

"Well, I'll be sure to tell Jack you stopped by," Elaine said, this time nearly shutting the door in his face.

"Wait, I'm here to pick Sunshine up for a date," Lou quickly pleaded.

"Oh, why didn't you say so?"

"I thought I just did."

"Very funny. She's staying in the guesthouse by the pool. Go around back and you'll find her there."

"It was nice meeting you."

"Likewise. Have fun, but don't keep our Sunshine out too late. She has to get up early. She's going with Jack to KTLA-TV to demonstrate some exercises live on air during their morning show."

"Don't worry, I'll have her home by midnight," and with that, he left.

"Well, don't you look nice? I've only seen you in shorts and without a shirt, so this is a pleasant surprise. Where are we going?" Sunshine wanted to know. Lou looked like he was dressed for a night on the town sporting a brown blazer with a burnt orange turtleneck, and polyester slacks.

"Since I've spent a lot of time over the past few years filming in Italy, I thought you might like to go to an Italian restaurant. Have you ever heard of Musso and Frank Grill?" Lou asked.

"Only that Hemingway and Fitzgerald dined there."

"And Bette Davis, Charlie Chaplin, and Greta Garbo."

"I read a lot of books so I'm more of a fan of authors than film stars."

"Yet you decided to go out with me."

"Well, you seem different. Do you read a lot?"

"No, but I love the opera," Lou answered.

"Me, too," Sunshine said.

"My lady, your chariot awaits," delivering the line much like he would in one of his Hercules movies.

"The way you said that reminded me of Steve Reeves. You kinda look like him, you know," Sunshine said in earnest.

"I thought you didn't go to movies," Lou said with a sly smile.

"I don't, but I've seen pictures of him in the magazines I used to sell."

"That's interesting. The reason I was signed to a three-picture deal was to compete with Steve Reeves. I think they thought I was the next Hercules—which I was.

So I'll take that as a compliment."

"It is a compliment." She hung on his arm as they walked past the pool and around the side of the house, hugging the walkway and perfectly manicured hedges. "That's your car. I love it," Sunshine said.

"It's a Fiat Spyder I bought while I was in Italy. I had it shipped over."

"Can we go topless? I mean… "

"I know what you mean," and he quickly removed the roof of the car.

"Boy, I thought Jack was on a strict diet, but you're really careful about what you eat," Sunshine said, no longer worried about offending Lou any more than she already had.

"You know what they say, you are what you eat," Lou replied.

"Then I guess I'm a saucy girl. That was delicious. Thank you, Lou."

"The night's not over yet, Sunshine—unless you want it to be," Lou said as the two drove along Sunset Boulevard.

"I'm having a great time. What do you want to do next?" Sunshine asked.

"How would you like to go to a movie studio?"

"Sure."

"Good because we're here."

They pulled up to the gate at the Warner Brothers Studios and were waved through by the guard who knew Lou. They parked near Studio 2 and headed for a back-stage entrance. Along the way Sunshine marveled at the re-creation of a New York City street lined with real trees, street lights, and signage that were so authentic she believed the buildings were real instead of being just facades.

"I'm here all the time because I'm a vocal coach for a few of the actors and I work with a lot of them on set or in their trailers."

"You lead an interesting life, Lou. Do you coach anyone I might know?"

"I'm not supposed to say, but yeah, you would know a few of them—that is if you went to the movies or watched television, which you said you don't."

"Hey, I go to the movies occasionally. I just prefer to live my life instead of watching others live theirs on a screen."

"Maybe someone will make a movie about you someday, Sunshine."

"So far, my life has been so strange, nobody would ever believe it. Like meeting you today. Now I'm here at a Hollywood studio after dinner at a restaurant filled with movie stars."

"It's only glamorous from the outside looking in. Once you've been in the industry for a while it's just like any other job... only it pays better," Lou said.

"Then why did you quit?" Sunshine wanted to know.

"When the spaghetti western replaced the sword-and-sandal stuff, the studios stopped calling, so I needed to find something to do after my last movie. At first, I started showing other actors how to build muscle and live a healthier lifestyle. It was just by chance that a well-known actor saw me sing tenor in an opera while we were both over in Italy. He asked if I would show him how to have more of a stage presence and improve his voice. That person told a few of his friends, who also happen to be famous, and that's how I became a vocal coach in Hollywood. Now I have a couple dozen clients and one of them is here tonight."

"Oh, who is it?"

"Dean Martin. He's Italian, you know. We Italians stick together."

"That's what I've heard."

"No, I mean he hired me even though he was already a huge star. He didn't have to do that, but he complained he was always copying the singing styles of others and now he wanted to develop his own sound so he could hold his own in duets with Sinatra. He also hired me to help his kids with their singing," Lou proudly stated.

"I didn't know Dean Martin had kids. He always seems so, I don't know, drunk," Sunshine blurted out.

"That's mostly just an act. He loves his kids and they have real talent, which is why he asked me to work with them."

They went into Studio 2 where *The Dean Martin Show* was being filmed and were escorted backstage. Sunshine was in awe when she got a glimpse of the set. It was a replica of the inside of a home and had furniture, a fireplace, bookcases, a balcony, and other decorative touches that made it look real except she could see the back of the walls which were just plywood.

Sunshine watched the show from the side of the stage and found herself laughing hysterically at the jokes and skits, which included stars she'd seen on the screen but didn't know their names until Lou pointed them out. During a break in filming Dean Martin made his way over to them.

"So, how's my singing soundin' tonight, ole buddy?" Dean wanted to know.

"I'd remind you to do your breathing exercises, but that would mean you would have to put your cigarette down for a few minutes and I know that's not gonna happen," Lou replied and gave a fake jab at Martin, who was once a boxer.

"Lou, Lou, Lou. If I stopped smoking I wouldn't know what to do with my hands, and then the ladies would be in big trouble."

"You mean bigger trouble. Speaking of ladies, let me introduce you to my date. Sunshine, meet Dino Crocetti."

"You can call me Dean. Nice to meet you, Sunshine. How do you like the show so far?"

"I love it."

"Good. Maybe NBC will keep me on the air for another year and I'll be able to continue to pay Lou for my singing lessons. Do you sing, Sunshine?"

"I don't always sing in the right key, but I always enjoy the song."

"Man, that's the story of my life," Martin replied with his signature self-deprecating humor.

Just then, "Les Brown and his Band of Renown" played the show's theme music, which meant it was time for Dean to get back to work, but not before he lit a fresh cigarette.

DEAR DIARY *I dated Lou for a few months and we had a great time together, but in the end, he wasn't right for me—or me for* *him. As much I was living a healthy lifestyle at the time, Lou took it a little too far. Through Lou I met some very interesting people—including a man I would later date.*

1967

HANGING OUT IN HOLLYWOOD

TWENTY-NINE YEARS OLD

"Look at how blue the water is. It's beautiful. Pull over. I want to go for a swim," Sunshine said, as her new boyfriend drove them down Pacific Coast Highway in his silver Porsche 550 Spyder convertible—the same car James Dean drove, which wasn't by coincidence.

"But I have a lunch meeting," he said, "and I thought you'd like to come along."

"It's Saturday, AJ. Take the day off and let's go to the beach," Sunshine pleaded as the white sand beckoned below.

"As the go-to doctor for Hollywood's biggest stars, I'm always on call. You know that."

"Fine. So who are we meeting for lunch?" Sunshine asked.

"Brando," her doctor boyfriend said matter-of-factly.

LEE SILBER

"As in Marlon Brando?"

"One and the same. That reminds me, try to not say anything about his weight."

"Why would I?"

"You'll see when we sit down to eat."

"Okay, but can I ask him about his films?" Sunshine asked.

"I don't see why not. I guess it's just like asking a normal person about what they do for a living," the doctor said. Then added, "The only thing is, nothing about Marlon is normal."

Sunshine and "Doc Hollywood," as he was known, pulled into the parking lot of a small diner located on Pacific Coast Highway and right across from the beach. There were only a couple of other cars in the parking lot and one of them was Marlon Brando's white Cadillac DeVille convertible. When they walked in, they saw a large man wearing a hat and sunglasses. If Sunshine didn't know they were meeting Marlon Brando, she would have thought it was just another patron. When Marlon spotted the doctor, he waved them over to his table.

"Sit, sit," the famous actor said.

"I hope you don't mind, but I brought my friend Sunshine along."

"Of course, of course," Brando said in his signature voice, and rose slightly to kiss her hand.

"You really know how to greet a girl," Sunshine said, blushing just a little.

"That's what all of my wives said… at first."

Sunshine looked at all of the food at the table and said, "You ordered for us?"

Doc Hollywood kicked her under the table, but Marlon Brando brushed it off and said, "Food is my weakness, right, Doc?"

"Well, let's see what we have here," the doctor said as he surveyed the table. "Bananas, that's good, except you covered them with cream. Corn flakes are okay, but it looks like that's your second bowl."

"You're killing me, Doc."

The doctor gave him a raised eyebrow as if to say, "Really?"

"I know, Doc, but I love food. The egg and sausage omelette here is to die for."

"Interesting choice of words, Marlon. Let me ask you something. Did you go to Pink's for hotdogs last night?" Something the actor was known to do.

"No."

"Good."

"I went there at three this morning," Brando said,

laughing at his own joke. "Can I help it if they're open all night?"

"Boys, boys," Sunshine said, "Can we please talk about something else?"

"I like her, Doc."

"So do I, so don't get any ideas," the doctor knew Brando had a weakness for food and the ladies—and not necessarily in that order.

"Hey, I'm married. So tell me, Sunshine, what do you do?" the movie star wanted to know.

"Everything, and nothing," Sunshine replied, meaning it just as it sounded.

"Tell me more," Brando said between bites.

"I just sold my cosmetics company," Sunshine said proudly.

"Why did you sell it?"

"When I started LaVie I was broke. All I had was an idea. That's when I met a man with a formula for using royal jelly in makeup to make a woman look and feel years younger. I met another man with money who wanted to start a business. I didn't know anything about cosmetics—I didn't even wear makeup at the time. All I had was an interesting idea and a will to succeed. So the three of us pulled it all together and the company took off almost right away. That's when we got an offer we couldn't refuse, and sold the company."

The waitress walked over to their table with a piece of apple pie and a glass of milk and Marlon tried to wave her away before she got to the table, but the waitress ignored him and set the dessert down in front of him anyway. Brando just shrugged.

"What can I get you two?" the waitress asked.

Sunshine and the Doc glanced at their menus and ordered sandwiches. During that short time, Brando had wolfed down the pie and was gulping down his milk.

Sunshine and the actor talked as if they were old friends—leaving the Doc out of the conversation, and looking uncomfortable. Sunshine couldn't believe a movie star was interested in her, but Brando wanted to know all about her unconventional life and his insightful questions drew her in. She could see why women loved him. He had the most amazing smile, almost like a smirk. He was intelligent as well as charming and charismatic. The two talked about everything *but* his acting career.

Finally, the doctor jumped into the conversation. "Did you know that to research a role Marlon once pretended to be paraplegic? He was so convincing the real patients at the hospital forced him to get up from his wheelchair and walk before they believed he wasn't really injured. He was that good."

"Doc, Sunshine here is a rare bird and probably bored by all this talk about me and my acting. I know I am."

"Okay, Marlon. At least tell her the story about the time you were in an acting class and the teacher told all the students to act like chickens hearing an air-raid siren."

Marlon sat back in the booth, crossed his arms and refused to speak. So the doctor spoke for him.

"You know what Marlon did?"

Sunshine shook her head no.

"Nothing. He just stood there while all the other actors flapped their arms and made crazy chicken sounds as if they were in grave danger. So when the teacher asked him what he was doing, Marlon said, 'I'm a chicken—I don't know what an air-raid siren is.'" The Doc laughed loudly. Sunshine wasn't sure what to do since Brando was giving her date the death stare. Brando slowly slid out of the booth and stood to leave.

"Aw, come on, Marlon. I love that story," the doctor said.

"It's alright. Hey, do you two want to join me and some friends for dinner and a show tonight? There's someone I want you to meet, Sunshine. I think you two will really hit it off."

The doctor, now feeling more than a little insecure, said, "Who's going?"

"My wife, my sister, Kim Novak, and a few others. We're meeting at the Brown Derby for dinner and then heading to the Hullabaloo to see an island band I just heard about."

"Sounds great, but I'm on call. Sorry."

"Sunshine, why don't you come along? I want you to meet Kim. She's going through a tough time and I think you would be good for her. I can have a driver pick you up from Doc's place."

"Sure. Sounds like fun."

The waitress came around with the bill and the doctor reached for his wallet. But Brando waved him off and handed the waitress a wad of cash.

"I'll be right back with your change?" she said.

"Keep the change, Dottie."

"Thank you, Marlon. That's very kind of you."

Hearing his name and putting two and two together, a man got up from the counter and walked over and said, "You're Marlon Brando. Would you sign my daughter's autograph book? I carry it with me in case I run into someone famous, and boy are you famous."

The Doc stepped in front of the man and said, "Mr. Brando doesn't sign autographs."

"It's okay, Doc," Marlon said and signed the man's autograph book. The Doc explained to Sunshine that

Marlon Brando's signature was so valuable people didn't cash his checks because his autograph was worth more than the check.

"See you tonight, Sunshine," Brando said and headed for the door.

The man at the counter looked down at the autograph book and said, "Mr. Brando, you signed it twice."

Marlon looked back and said with a smirk, "I heard that one John Wayne autograph was equal to two of mine on the collector's market, so I signed it twice."

DEAR DIARY *I did go to dinner with Marlon Brando and his friends that night—some of them famous actors like Karl Malden and Elizabeth Taylor—and he was right, Kim Novak was there and we became fast friends. We had a lot in common. Like me, she suffered a severe personal loss when a mudslide destroyed her Bel Air home and everything in it. She was also suddenly single after a divorce from her husband and I was recently widowed... or so I thought. We both loved poetry, art, and music—Kim created it and I admired it. She wanted to stay out of the spotlight and live a more normal life, and I had time on my hands so we palled around together. One of our favorite things to do was spend time at Santa Anita Park. We first went there to look at the thoroughbreds and the beautiful grounds, but then found it fun to bet on the races. Kim moved to Big Sur and started acting again in the late 1960s, and I relocated to Mexico so* we lost touch for a while, but over the years we remained pen pals.

One thing that always struck me about my time socializing with some of the biggest stars in Hollywood was how unhappy many of them were. They had a degree of fortune and fame that was unfathomable, yet they were still miserable. I wanted to say, "What's wrong with you people?" Instead of envy, I felt sorry for them. When you grow up poor like I did you appreciate things a lot more. To me, if you have the basics, you should be happy. These people had everything and then some. I saw a lot of excess from some of these stars, including the abuse of drugs and alcohol. For me, the only feeling better than the satisfaction that comes from earning something on your own is helping others get what they want and need.

1969

FROM MEXICO TO
THE MIDDLE OF NOWHERE

THIRTY-ONE YEARS OLD

Sunshine and her young son moved to Mexico City and then to Acapulco, staying at the luxurious Princess Hotel. Located right on the beach, the resort featured an enormous pool that went winding through the lush property, feeding into a cascading waterfall surrounded by palm trees. The hotel was shaped like a large Mayan pyramid and was a marvel to behold. Inside, the lobby was dominated by a tremendous atrium with balconies all around overlooking the courtyard below. The lobby level of the Princess featured fancy shops catering to the needs of their high-class clients.

The owner of the hotel was a man named Daniel Ludwig, a multimillionaire, who made his fortune selling paper produced in Brazil. His representative at the hotel was Warren Brogli, with whom Sunshine had become fast friends. Sunshine was also well acquainted with Pierre Jacy, a famous hair stylist from France who owned shops all over the world—and who was enjoying an extended stay at the hotel. It was over breakfast with these two powerful men that a plan began to formulate. With Sunshine's background in cosmetics and Pierre's success with salons, Warren Brogli suggested the two team up to open a spa and salon along with several related retail shops inside the Princess Hotel. Pierre would oversee the set-up and opening, while Sunshine would stay on to manage and maintain the business.

The only obstacle was a mandatory face-to-face meeting with Mr. Ludwig—the owner of the hotel—to discuss the details. Since the multimillionaire was a man on the go, Sunshine and Pierre agreed to fly to New York to close the deal. When they arrived in the city, Ludwig had already left for Amsterdam and asked if they wouldn't mind meeting him there—so they did. Finally, the three met up to make the deal.

Besides being a fabulous hair stylist, Pierre was also a shrewd businessman, and he didn't find the hotelier's offer lucrative enough for him to move to Mexico and open a salon at the Princess, so he passed and returned to Paris. With her son safely in boarding school, Sunshine decided to remain in Amsterdam to take in the sights. A fan of the opera, Sunshine saw several shows and while waiting for one to start, stopped in at a nearby bar in the late afternoon and met a man who would change her life forever.

Over drinks the two strangers got to know one another, and they discovered they had a lot in common—even though the man lived in Morocco. Like Sunshine, Salah loved the opera, was always traveling, enjoyed talking about business, and thrived on meeting new people. They both felt a strong connection, but at the end of the night they went their separate ways, but not before Salah said to Sunshine, "If you ever find yourself in Morocco, look me up." Little did he know she would take him up on his offer.

Sunshine walked into the travel agency located near her hotel in Paris and wondered, where do people who live in such a beautiful place go on vacation? Glancing around the office at the posters of exotic locales—a few she had already been to and several she would love to visit—she got the impression Parisians preferred tropical vacations. Instead, Sunshine sat down next to a tiny desk and announced, "I would like to purchase a plane ticket to Morocco."

Brigitte, the young travel agent, who looked like a model out of one of the fashion magazines, replied in broken English, "Are you sure you want to go there?"

"Yes, I met a man who lives there and—" Sunshine started before she was interrupted by the travel agent.

"Oh, so this is about love," the agent said.

"Well, uh, not exactly," Sunshine replied.

"Is this not your boyfriend you are going to see?"

"No, um… no. We just met."

"Oh, love at first sight. How romantic."

"Yes, I guess it is."

"And whom are you traveling to Morocco with? A brother perhaps?"

"I'm going alone," Sunshine said, not knowing how silly that sounded.

"Oh. Please wait here. I want to get my, how do you say, directeur?"

"Your boss?"

"Yes, my boss. Please wait."

A few minutes later an attractive older woman walked up with her hand outstretched and said, "Bonjour, my name is Antoinette. I am the owner of this agency. I hear you are interested in traveling to Morocco alone. I must warn you, this is not a good thing."

"Why?"

"Morocco is not a place to go if you are a woman—especially alone. In an Arab man's eyes you are worthless, less than human. When they see a beautiful blonde American like yourself traveling alone, they will likely try to drug you so they can kidnap you to sell as a slave or trade for camels. It's very, very dangerous. How about a nice trip to Tahiti instead?"

"No, I'll take my chances in Morocco. I have a good feeling about it."

"She has a good feeling about it," Antoinette said aloud. "Okay, but don't say I didn't warn you. Brigitte, go ahead and book the flight."

"Where exactly in Morocco do you want to go?"

Sunshine opened her purse and pulled out a piece of paper with the name of the place Salah said he lived and said, "I want to go to Agadir."

The travel agent let out a big breath of air and began the process of putting together a travel plan that had Sunshine flying from Paris-Le Bourget Airport to Madrid, then Casablanca, ending in Agadir. It was a series of short but potentially dangerous flights the agent reluctantly booked for Sunshine. After Brigitte was done she asked Sunshine, "Do you need a hotel in Agadir? I can call and reserve a room for you."

77

"Yes, that would be wonderful," Sunshine agreed. Wondering, just for the moment, if she wasn't crazy for making the trip. She decided, there are no accidents. Salah came into her life for a reason, and she wanted to find out what the reason was no matter what happened. Where she would end up is where we she was supposed to be all along. So she had no fear, at least not yet.

Sunshine was seated in the first-class section of the airplane and quickly noticed as the other passengers boarded that she was the only woman on the flight. As the Arab men paraded past she got the distinct impression she was not welcome and should watch her back. Once the plane was in the air the flight attendant offered her a meal. She was starving so she accepted and quickly devoured the delicious dish. However, she soon realized nobody else was eating and remembered—probably too late—that her meal may have been laced with a drug. She turned to the man seated next to her and asked him why he was not eating. He mumbled only one word, "Ramadan," and then ignored her the rest of the flight. (Sunshine later learned that Arab men do not eat during the day when it's Ramadan.) Sunshine nervously waited for the effects of the drugs to kick in while the plane traveled toward the Casablanca airport.

She did fall asleep, not because she was drugged but because she was exhausted. Sunshine was awakened by the steward who informed her she needed to get off the plane and go through customs. Once she disembarked, it was apparent she was the only woman in line and the men—most dressed in traditional garb—were not happy about having a female among them and they let her know with their contempt. Sunshine was extremely nervous, but she had no choice but to soldier on, so she did.

The next flight was on a much smaller (and older) plane. The cabin was filled with cigarette smoke due to the passengers' tendency to light a fresh cigarette from the previous one—and the lack of ventilation. It wasn't a short flight from Casablanca to Agadir, and despite the stench of smoke and sweat, she survived. Her spirits rose as the plane descended over what looked like a coastal town in Southern California—only it was Morocco. There were long stretches of white sand beaches and a beautiful cove with bright blue water. This was not at all the way she pictured this place in her mind, but she was relieved it looked familiar. It reminded her a little of Malibu. The plane continued inland and approached a cow pasture with a landing strip. Sadly, this was more what she imagined Agadir would look like.

After a very rough landing, Sunshine wobbled out

of the airplane and headed toward the only building in sight, a small cement structure in the middle of nowhere. Inside there was one big room with a small barrier in the middle. From the other side of the barrier several Arab men rushed toward her screaming at her in Arabic. Petrified, Sunshine grabbed a pole and held on for dear life as the men surrounded her—each one screaming louder than the other. The most aggressive man in the group grabbed her passport and hotel reservation out of her hand and promptly tore her paperwork into little pieces and threw them in the air and waved her passport over his head.

Sunshine was now hysterical and screamed, "Leave me alone! Help!"

The Airport Manager immediately came to her defense, running toward Sunshine and her attackers while shouting back at them in Arabic, which did the trick. The mob disbanded, but clearly, they were not happy about it.

The man handed Sunshine her passport back and said, "I'm so sorry about that. They tend to do that from time to time."

"Why?" Sunshine stammered back.

"Oh, it's simple. They are the taxi drivers and you were the only fare to arrive today."

"Why did they rip up my hotel confirmation?"

"Your hotel isn't ready yet, it's still under construction."

"Where will I stay then?"

"Not to worry. My family owns a hotel in south Agadir. If you would like, I can take you there. It's about an hour's drive from here. My name is Karim. What is yours?"

"Sunshine."

"Oh, I like that name." Karim said with a smile. "It's a very nice name. You must come with me and stay in south Agadir. It is lovely there, you will see."

Wary of strangers in a strange country, Sunshine said she would think about his offer while she went through customs. However, rather than have her wait in line, Karim used his position as Airport Manager to help Sunshine whip through the paperwork to get her passport stamped.

Karim also reiterated his offer to take her to his family's hotel on the coast. "I'm just about to get off work and live near the hotel, so it's no trouble at all to drive you there. We don't meet many Americans, so I know everyone will be excited to have you visit our village."

The man did sort of save her life, and he seemed nice enough. Sunshine didn't know where Salah lived—or even his last name—so she agreed to accept the offer of a ride and a place to stay… for now. They walked out of the airport together and made their way to the parking lot which was nearly empty except for a couple of cars.

"Karim, I love your car."

"Thank you, it's a Citroen, from France. Here, your luggage will fit in the back seat."

"Is it just us?"

"Yes, I drive a great distance every day for work. My wife stays at home with the children."

"I see. So you aren't planning to trade me for 47 camels?"

"What would I do with so many camels? Please relax. I'll show you the sights and tell you all about Agadir on our way to my hometown."

On the drive down Karim shared some of the local customs, pointed out places that had not yet been rebuilt after the enormous earthquake that devastated the region just ten years earlier. Then he talked at length about soccer—which Sunshine knew very little about, but she listened intently since Karim was so passionate about the sport.

It turned out Karim was also a very good listener and he was enthralled by Sunshine's adventurous life—including coming to Morocco to meet up with a man she hardly knew. By the time they arrived at the tiny town Karim called home he had invited Sunshine to stay with him and his family, and vowed to help her find Salah—which he did, but not in the way she thought.

It turned out Sunshine was a celebrity and big hit with Karim's family and friends. After staying at his home for a short while, the locals decided to throw a party in her honor. When word got out there was a big happening in honor of an American woman—a rarity in this region—Salah heard about it and put two and two together, and that's when he found the love of his life living just one town over.

DEAR DIARY *I was terrified the whole time I traveled to Morocco after the warning from the travel agent. I really believed nobody was eating any food on the plane because it was either tainted or drugged. I guess it could have been, but it wasn't—I only thought it was. I had never heard of Ramadan and the customs that go with it (to not eat during the day).*

Later that day when I was attacked by an angry mob of Arab men at the Agadir Airport, I assumed they were there to do me harm—grab me and make me a slave, or trade me for 47 camels. (That's the actual number of camels the travel agent felt I might go for on the open market. Interesting.) Yet when I learned they were simply cab drivers desperate for a fare and meant me no harm, the whole thing seems rather silly now. The lesson I learned is that when you know what's going on, things are a lot less scary.

And even if you don't know what's really going on, have faith that things will work out. If Karim lived north of the airport, I may never have met back up with Salah, who also just so happened to live in the south of Agadir.

My son was safe where he was—at boarding school and with relatives—and there was no way I would have ever brought him along on this trip. In fact, for most of his young life Shawn was better off being cared for by others. It was hard to leave him behind, but I knew it was for the best for both of us.

1970

MARRIED IN MOROCCO

THIRTY-TWO YEARS OLD

The first time Sunshine married, she did it for lust. This time, it would be for love. Some would see it as her marrying for money—since Salah made millions of dollars in international banking to go along with his family's existing wealth. He lived like a prince and Sunshine was treated like a princess. If this were anywhere but Morocco, it would be many a woman's dream to live a life of luxury in a palace complete with servants, gourmet meals, and access to a private plane. Sunshine had an entire wing of the property to herself, which was decorated with exotic and expensive furniture, rare rugs, a giant canopy bed, and art from around the world. It was opulent and ornate. Her closet was filled with designer clothes and the walls were lined with books by her favorite authors. All of this, and she still felt trapped. Sunshine wasn't allowed to leave the compound unless she was accompanied by her husband, a member of the family, or someone from the staff.

When the couple was together—which wasn't often enough since Salah was away on business more than he was home, her new life in a foreign land was a dream come true. Sunshine wanted for nothing, and she and her fiancé were very happy when they were home alone—which was a rarity with Salah's family and friends coming and going day and night. The lovestruck couple was convinced it was fate that brought them together, but neither would have guessed that faith could tear them apart. They believed their love for one another could conquer all. They were united despite pressure from Salah's inner circle to convert the strong-willed Sunshine to a Muslim way of life—something she was unwilling to do.

Sunshine wore clothes suited for the culture and climate—even covering her head when she went out in public. She looked more like a movie star playing the part of an American living abroad—which she was—than a true native of the Arab nation. At times, she would sneak out and walk to the six-mile stretch of beach that made Agadir so popular (it looked a lot like Southern California except for the people riding camels on the beach.) She didn't dare jump in the Atlantic for fear someone would see her in her bikini and tell someone in Salah's family. The family already frowned on Salah for allowing her to mix and mingle with his friends—many of these men were high-ranking officials—and spend time in the drinking room as their equal, which in the family's eyes, she was not.

Since Sunshine was not Moroccan, not Muslim, and not a virgin, that was three strikes against her. Also, the family didn't feel she was worthy of marriage or motherhood with their eldest son—two things the couple both wanted. Salah stood up for her when he was there, but Sunshine was subjected to all sorts of verbal abuse when he wasn't around. Salah's family and friends called her every name in the book in their native tongue, some of which she understood, the rest she translated later using a book in her private library to convert Arabic to English. Nobody knew she was able to understand what they were saying so they spoke freely in her presence and much of what they said made her fear for her safety.

The mansion was built into the side of the mountain and blended in since the clay color of the walls and buildings matched the surrounding area—which were barren hills except for the palm trees planted inside the gated compound. Since the family owned the land as far as the eye could see, they left it undeveloped. A high wall with turrets made up the perimeter and Salah's private security force manned the gate, letting nobody in or out unless authorized by the family—this included Sunshine.

Fortunately, the wing of the palace Sunshine's private room was located in was in the back corner of the property and featured an outdoor patio area that backed up to a row of trees and a hill full of boulders. There was no wall there since it wasn't near the road and the boulders and trees behind her room provided privacy and served as a natural barrier. It didn't take long for Sunshine to slip away and hike up the hill—and then explore deeper into the open area away from prying eyes. Each day she would escape deeper and deeper into the valleys until she found the most amazing place on earth.

To remain out of sight during her deep forays into the deserted hills behind the house, she stayed in the crevices carved out of the mountains by water. The foliage provided shade (and cover) and following the streams kept her from getting lost. Making her way through a crack in the cliffs Sunshine stumbled on a large pool of crystal clear water. The feeling she felt when she first saw this pristine place was one of pure joy. This was her place. It was nearly impossible to find and was surrounded on all sides by tall cliffs, and it was on private property—Salah's property. She didn't want to leave—

yet she had to before someone at the palace noticed she was missing.

The day after her discovery of this magical spot, she returned with a bathing suit and towel. Without a soul in sight or a sound to be heard, Sunshine stripped down to her bikini and jumped in the warm water and floated on her back looking at a cloudless sky and the features of the tall cliffs above. She had never known or felt such peace. This was her favorite place and somewhere she would try to come to whenever she could sneak away. After swimming, she stretched out on the sand around the edge of the water to soak in the sun, not a care in the world.

"I want you to keep a closer eye on Salah's woman when he's not here," Sofian, Salah's younger brother said to the head of security.

"You want me to spy on her?" Omar asked.

"Did I say that?"

"I think you just did."

"Call it what you will. I suspect this woman is leaving the compound during the day and I want to know where she goes," Sofian said.

"I'm guessing you want me to report back to you and not Salah," Omar said, grinning just a little.

"Nobody likes a smart aleck, Omar."

"Okay, but if I get caught, your brother will have my head for spying on his woman."

"So don't get caught," Sofian said.

"I'll do my best," was Omar's reply.

"You were in the Army, Omar. Didn't they train you how to track a person without being seen or heard?"

"Of course. Don't worry, I'll handle it."

"That's what I want to hear. I'll be eager to learn what you find out. Keep me posted."

"Of course, sir."

The next day, Omar was perched on the roof of the palace with a pair of binoculars and a walkie-talkie. From this vantage point, he had a clear view of the entire property. If Sunshine left the compound, he would be able to see where she went and order one of his underlings to follow her by car and report back. Then he would be ready for the trickier type of tailing that happens at close range.

To Omar's surprise, his subject left out of her back door and disappeared behind the trees. He didn't expect this and had to scramble down from his post to be in a position to pursue Sunshine into the hills on the open side of the property. There were several possible paths, so he would have to guess right or wait until she left the grounds another day.

By now, Sunshine had her routine down and could make it to her secret spot in under half an hour—and considering the scorching sun, any longer and she would not find the hike quite as enjoyable. Her perfect pond was worth the effort—and would be even if it took her twice as long to get there.

So far, nobody in the family was the wiser about her daily field trips into the desert, but she worried if she stayed away too long someone would notice her absence. Fortunately, the mansion had so many rooms she could say she was in an area of the palace that the family and servants don't frequent and it would be believable.

The time she spent hiking and swimming was important for her sanity, and her safety. With Salah gone, she was starting to feel like nobody wanted her there, and she often wondered if someone might do something to make her want to pack up and leave—or worse, just make her disappear.

As she approached the valley where her secret spot was, the trail narrowed and vegetation—including beautiful blooming flowers—lined the path. She could hear the small waterfall off to the left, which fed into a smaller stream not suitable for swimming. For the past few trips to the perfect pond, Sunshine set her shoes and clothes on an outcropping of rocks and jumped 15 feet into the translucent water (which was plenty deep).

After a long swim, Sunshine stretched out on a flat rock and fell asleep as the hot sun baked her skin. She was startled and awakened suddenly from one of the peaceful dreams she always had while napping here. By now, she knew all of the natural sounds in the area, and something wasn't right. Trickling down from the cliffs above were small rocks and sand. Shielding her eyes, Sunshine looked up and was blinded by a bright light. It was the reflection of the sun off something very shiny. Her heart sank and her stomach did a flip when she was able to better focus. It was a man with a pair of binoculars looking down at her. She instinctively covered up with a towel and then put on her shoes, scooped up her belongings, and chased after him. There was only one way in and out of the valley and she was going to cut him off and confront him. This was private property, after all.

When Omar realized that his quarry had not only seen him but was coming after him, he decided to make a run for it—only he lost his footing and started sliding down the cliff on his rear end. His fear got the better of him and he screamed as he slid, tumbled, and was mercifully launched from an outcropping of rocks into the air. He seemed to float for a few seconds until he landed face first in the water below.

If Omar wasn't panicked before, he was now—he didn't know how to swim. He ignored the pain to nearly every part of his body and instead focused on his survival. Instantly he was underwater and sinking fast. If he wasn't fighting for his life, it was a beautiful view with the sun's rays shining down from above. He could make out the cliffs and the palm trees and wished he was up there instead of down here. Frantically, he moved his arms and legs but seemed to be sinking deeper and deeper into the clear water. There was a sharp pain and ringing in his ears and a burning sensation in his lungs. When he hit the water, he must have had the wind knocked out of him because his reflexes made him want to try to breathe underwater, but he knew better. Looking up and not being able to move up was infuriating and frustrating. His robe and sandals were like an anchor dragging him down, so he kicked them off. He thought maybe he was making more progress toward the surface, but at the rate he was ascending, he knew he wouldn't make it. A strange calm came over him as he let the blackness close in around him. This was not how he thought he would die.

Sunshine didn't hesitate for one second. She dove in to save the man who minutes ago she worried was there to spy on her—or worse, kill her. She only knew one way to live, and that was to do the right thing no matter what. By the time she reached the man he was almost at the bottom of the pond, over twenty feet deep. With the clarity of the water, he was easy to find, but hauling him to the surface was awkward—especially since he wasn't wearing any clothes.

Once Sunshine was finally able to drag the man up on the small beach that surrounded the pool of water, she began performing mouth-to-mouth resuscitation on him. She worried he had been down a long time and that it might be too late to save him, but she had to try. Suddenly, the man began coughing up water and did so for a full two minutes. Now on his hands and knees, the man seemed to grasp the gravity of the situation—he was naked and Sunshine had just saved his life.

That's when the man blurted out, "My clothes, I need my clothes." He did his best to cover up as he said it, but it was still uncomfortable for both of them.

"You want me to dive down and bring up your clothes?" Sunshine asked.

"Don't you know how to swim?" the man asked.

"I do it all the time," Sunshine said. "You should

know, you were spying on me."

"I, uh, yes, please, I beg you, my robe," he said in broken English. "I cannot go back without it. My sandals, too, if you can find them."

Sunshine rolled her eyes, "Fine. But how about a thank you for saving your life?"

"*You* saved me?"

"Do you see anyone else around?" Sunshine asked with her arms outstretched.

"No, it can't be. If this is true, then thank you. I am forever in your debt."

"It's okay, you don't owe me anything. You would have done the same for me, that is, if you could swim."

"I promise to learn to swim someday, but for now, could you *please* get my clothes?"

Sunshine managed to find one sandal, a pair of boxer shorts, and a robe after several deep dives, and presented it to the naked man curled up on the beach. "This is all I could find," she said, presenting him with his clothes while trying to not laugh at his camel print underwear.

"I am most grateful. Thank you, Sunshine."

"So, you know my name?"

"You are just such a bright light, I figured your name must be Sunshine."

"Cut the crap. You followed me here from the house.

I want to know why."

"If I tell you that, I could be in big trouble."

"Spill it. If I tell Salah what happened here today, which one of us do you think he will be most mad at?"

"Please don't tell Salah about this most unfortunate incident."

"Fine, then tell me who sent you."

"Sofian sent me. He wanted to know where you go when you leave your room."

Sunshine was mad at herself for not being more careful about her movements. Salah could care less that she went hiking and swimming on the property, but his brother would surely use this against her. With their wedding day only a few weeks away, the family was trying extra hard to make her life miserable in the hopes she would crack and call off the ceremony. Not a chance.

"What's *your* name?"

"My name is Omar, and I am head of security for the family."

"How come we've never met before?"

"Salah wants you to feel safe, but he also doesn't want you to feel like you are a prisoner, so I was ordered to guard you from afar," Omar said with a thick accent.

"I see. How about we make a deal? Just between you and me."

"I don't know."

"What about you being forever in my debt? You know, after I saved your life and all."

"Fine, what do you have in mind?"

Sunshine and Omar struck a deal for each other's silence and they promised to help one another if either needed assistance in the future. It was a deal that would prove to be a lifesaver for Sunshine.

DEAR DIARY *To me, freedom is a lot more valuable than possessions and wealth—and happiness trumps everything. Living like a princess in Morocco was wonderful at times, but I had no freedom and ultimately, I was unhappy. When I looked around my room all I saw were things. They were expensive things, but they brought me no joy. My hikes to my sacred pool in the hills behind the house were some of the best days of my life and they cost nothing. I find that an exciting or enlightening experience is more fulfilling than expensive items. I believe we are the sum total of our experiences. The more experiences we have, the more we are able to deal with things and the richer we are for them.*

When Salah was away I felt lonely and trapped in the palace and really had nobody to talk to. His parents and brother gave me the silent treatment and the servants were all too afraid to talk to me. I'm a social person by nature and I need human interaction like I need food and water. It's ironic that what led me to Morocco and my future husband was my willingness to talk to anyone, anywhere. I never liked dining alone, drinking alone, or being alone. That's why I never passed up an opportunity to talk to a stranger. There are no accidents. The person sitting next to you on a plane or train is there for a reason. I really believe that.

1971

MOM ON THE RUN

THIRTY-THREE YEARS OLD

Salah and Sunshine snuggled in their seats on a private plane heading for their long-awaited honeymoon in Mexico. Sunshine chose Acapulco for their extended vacation because it also gave and her chance to spend the summer with Shawn since boarding school ended in less than a week.

"You have no idea how happy you made my parents by agreeing to a traditional Moroccan wedding ceremony," Salah said as he kissed his new wife on the cheek.

"It was an amazing experience. I'm glad we did it that way. The food, the music, and all the decorations. It must have cost a fortune," Sunshine said as she squeezed her husband's hand.

"You're worth it," Salah replied. "But you forgot to mention your wedding gown. You looked stunning in it.

All the ladies were envious of you."

"They should be. I just married the most amazing man in Agadir," Sunshine said, and then kissed him back.

"It's a small town," Salah joked.

"And it did seem like the entire town came to the wedding. I didn't know most of the people there."

"You're one of us now, Mrs. Benrahheth."

"Wow, it's going to take a little while to get used to using your last name."

"It's our last name. It's also a name that's well-respected in Agadir. It opens a lot of doors."

"So we're staying in Morocco?" Sunshine asked.

"Yes, that will be where we live and raise a family, but we'll travel, too."

Sunshine nodded and asked, "Speaking of family, did everyone at the wedding ask you when we were going to start a family of our own?"

"Just my parents, why?"

"I don't know. It seemed like everyone wanted to know when I would be pregnant, but I'm not sure they were asking because they were happy about it."

"Come on, you're imagining things, Sunshine. Don't think about it. We're going to be away from Morocco for over a month in beautiful Acapulco, let's just focus on us. Who knows, maybe we will come back with some good news on the baby front. You never know."

As fate would have it, shortly after the happy couple returned from their extended honeymoon, Sunshine found out she was pregnant—and her worst fears were realized.

Sunshine wanted to wait a while before telling Salah's family that the couple was expecting. If it was to be a boy, he would be the first born son of the first born son. Not realizing at the time what this would mean for her and the baby, Sunshine went along with Salah's wishes and agreed to tell the family the good news.

Right away things went from bad to worse with Salah's family and friends. They all assumed the baby would be a boy and he would be raised as a Muslim in Morocco. This meant the family had to teach (more like force and enforce) the rules of the religion and the region so Salah's new bride could become one of them. They insisted Sunshine wear a Jilbab at all times and read the Koran, which she reluctantly did. It was critical (in their minds) that Sunshine convert and give up her rights as an American and as a woman. Unfortunately, Salah often sided with his family when it came to what it meant to be the wife and mother of a Moroccan Muslim. She was scared of what would become of her and her baby—but she only had one person she could confide in, and she wasn't sure even he could be trusted, despite saving his life and their agreement to help one another, no questions asked.

Omar and Sunshine often swam side by side in the sacred pool. As partial payment for not revealing this special place to Salah's brother, she agreed to teach him how to swim—and now that's all Omar wanted to do—even if he insisted on swimming in his thobe (a long white robe most Muslim men in Morocco wore).

"Omar, do you remember how I was treated before the wedding and when I got pregnant?" Omar shrugged his shoulders, but didn't say a word, so Sunshine answered for him. "They treated me pretty badly. You know that, right?"

Again, Omar remained mum, so Sunshine continued answering her own questions. "I know you know they treat me like dirt. Less than dirt, actually. I'm sure the others in the house are saying horrible things about me. I can't understand them when they speak in Arabic or French, but I can tell. It's like I'm a prisoner and gave up my rights as an American woman—but I didn't. Right?"

This time Omar replied, "When you married Salah, you did give up your freedom. You did not realize this?"

"No. I just assumed things would be the same

as they were before the wedding, but everything's changed—even Salah."

"You should not have assumed. The baby will be born here and will be a citizen of Morocco. That's how it works," Omar informed her.

"That is not going to happen," Sunshine said as she exited the water and walked a short distance to her towel and Burqa, which she reluctantly wore when outside just in case someone saw her. Not only was this head-to-toe traditional garment constricting, it was also extremely uncomfortable in the hot sun.

"You don't have a choice. It is what it is, as you often say."

"Oh, I have a choice, and I choose freedom for myself and my baby."

"Please tell me you are not thinking of leaving Morocco."

"Okay, I won't tell you that, but it's what I plan to do, I just can't do it alone. I need help."

"What about Karim, your friend from the airport. Didn't he help you get into the country? Maybe he can help you get out, too?" Omar said with a look that led Sunshine to believe he didn't want to help her escape— which didn't stop her from asking for his assistance.

"Omar, to pull this off I'm going to need your

help, too."

At this point Omar dropped to his knees and started praying, so Sunshine left him there and began the hike back to the house. She knew he would come around. For her plan to work, he would have to.

Sunshine sat at a large fancy desk in the library room of the palace. It was complete with a set of atlases containing detailed maps of the area. Plotting her escape was tricky. To the north of Agadir was Marrakesh, but the city was inland and far too dangerous a bus ride for a friend like Karim. The city was famous for welcoming westerners and a Mecca for hippies and hipsters, but getting there would be almost impossible without a car. To the south were several small towns, but none with an airport.

This meant she would have to persuade Salah to let her leave, which meant he might become suspicious of her true intentions—but it was a risk she would have to take. Sunshine came up with all kinds of clever reasons why she wanted to leave the country—including flying with her husband on business, but he insisted she stay in Morocco until the baby was born. Weeks and then months passed as Sunshine came up with a dozen different plans to get away, but none panned out. Nearly eight months pregnant she was desperate, and willing to try anything to make it to America before the baby was born. It was now or never, so Sunshine decided to risk everything for freedom.

"All I'm asking you to do is look the other way, Omar. You don't have to do anything else, just let me leave."

"If the family finds out I helped you escape, do you know what they will do to me?"

"No."

"I don't know either, but it won't be good. They could have me thrown in jail, or worse. Please, I beg you, don't do this."

"Omar, have you forgotten that it was me who pulled you up from the deepest part of the pond and then breathed life back into you?"

"I know what you did for me. But did you save me just to have me killed a year later?"

"It won't come to that, I promise. You will be able to say you knew nothing of my plan to escape from the palace, since I won't tell you how I'll do it."

"Thanks, I think."

"Don't thank me yet. All you have to do is act natural and respond as you normally would to an emergency in the house."

"What emergency?"

"You'll know it when it happens."

"Oh no, this is not good."

"I agree, it's not good, it's great. Trust me, it'll work."

"Do I have a choice?"

"Not really. It's happening whether you like it or not, so why not play your part and pretend like everything is normal—until it isn't."

"I have no idea what you are talking about."

"See, you know nothing, so you have nothing to fear."

"If you say so."

"Where will you go once you are out of the country?" Omar asked.

"The less you know, the better."

The night before her escape, Sunshine couldn't sleep. There were so many things that could go wrong with her plan and she would be stuck in this golden cage forever, plus she would probably be punished for trying to run away.

Over the past few months Sunshine was able to set aside some money, but she would need much more than she was able to cobble together. So, she gathered up all of the expensive jewelry she could get her hands on (most of the items were gifts from Salah, and some were wedding presents) and grabbed a couple of other small things of value that she could possibly trade for favors.

Although she wasn't required to completely cover herself when inside, Sunshine began doing so in anticipation of her escape. Her Burqa made her invisible and allowed her to move about unnoticed. She could also hide a few items she would need to take with her—including regular clothes she would wear once out of the country. Sunshine found a burqa in the laundry room that was two sizes too big hoping it hid the fact she was very pregnant. Now with her plan in place and less than an hour until she would leave, she laid on the bed waiting for everyone else to fall asleep.

Somewhere in the house her passport was hidden, but after weeks of searching the expansive property, she was unable to find it. In a way that was a good thing, because she now knew where it wasn't kept. There was only one place she had yet to look, but before now it was too risky to look for it in Salah's brother's room. Now she had nothing left to lose. Without her passport, her whole plan would go up in smoke—much like she planned to do to the kitchen in a matter of minutes. There was no turning back now.

"Fire! There is a fire in the kitchen. Everyone wake up!' Omar yelled as he ran through the corridors of the massive house, all the while thinking there had to be a more subtle way Sunshine could have used to create a diversion for her escape. This stunt could end up burning the entire palace to the ground.

Sofian came running from his room, "Omar, what is it? What's happening?"

"There's a fire in the kitchen. Call the fire brigade and I'll make sure everyone gets out safely."

"My parents," Sofian yelled, ready to run in the opposite direction.

"Call in the fire from their room," Omar said. "It's the farthest from the kitchen and safe... for now. Go. I'll handle everything here."

Smoke billowed out of the kitchen and Omar began banging on doors to do what he said he would, wake everyone up and lead them to safety. As he passed Sofian's open door, he pretended not to see Sunshine hiding behind a large plant down the hall. At least that was one less person he wouldn't have to find and save.

Sunshine knew she didn't have much time. She needed to find her passport quickly and escape out the back of the house. Omar would almost certainly lead everyone out the front of the house where the fire brigade would also enter the residence. This would cause so much commotion she would be able to return to her room and slip out the back patio to the familiar paths she'd hiked so many times over the past year. She wanted to see her special place one last time before leaving. She would have to navigate in the dark, but since it was a full moon (part of the plan) she could get there in an hour. If everything went right, she would be able to hide in the hills until light and then make her way to meet Karim who would drive her to the airport. But first she had to find her passport.

The door to Sofian's room was open, so Sunshine slipped in and using a flashlight from the kitchen, went straight to the large desk in the living room of his wing of the home. Her hands were shaking so severely from fear, Sunshine found it difficult to search, but luckily her passport was right where she thought it would be. With her passport in hand, Sunshine searched around for any cash she could find to help her pay Karim for his help, but decided against it since any money she took would be stealing, something she was unwilling to do.

The fire Sunshine set in the kitchen was only supposed to be a small, isolated one that could easily be extinguished. As she passed the kitchen on her way back to her part of the palace, she could feel the heat and the smoke burned her eyes. Part of her wanted to help put it out, but she knew what she had to do and that was get out of the house as soon as possible.

Sunshine made her way to the back of the palace she had called home for over a year and grabbed a bag that held everything she needed to take with her. She wanted to take much more, but in the end she chose to travel light and leave with essentially what she'd arrived with. The most precious thing she was taking with her was also the most bulky, the baby in her belly. It wouldn't be easy to hike the hills in the dark at eight months pregnant—and she worried the anxiety and excitement could cause her to go into labor prematurely—but she believed what she was doing was the right thing and knew in her heart that everything would work out. It had to.

Watching the moonlight dance on the water of the sacred pond, she regretted she had never come here at night before. It wasn't the only regret she was grappling with. Sunshine wondered what Salah would do once he learned of her escape—and the fact she set part of his home on fire. Maybe she should have just stuck it out and had the baby here, leaving later when he was older. However, she knew the family would never let that happen. She even wondered if Salah would ever let her leave Morocco with their son. It was too late to have regrets, she had to stay focused because she wasn't out of the woods, yet. Far from it.

Later, Karim was waiting in his trusty blue Citroen on a dirt road seemingly in the middle of nowhere. The reason Sunshine picked this meeting place was that it was hard to find, but easy to get to from the pond. Even if the family sent the police or their security people to look for her, it was very unlikely they would look here. Her biggest fear was Karim wouldn't find it either. So Sunshine and Karim did a trial run a few weeks earlier. She called her friend and told him to get a copy of an Atlas and find the spot by studying the landmarks on the map and by using the coordinates she provided over the phone. He was right where he was supposed to be, and as the sun rose up from the desert floor and behind the mountains, Sunshine could see Karim's car and she began her descent down from her hiding place up on the hill.

Karim got out of the car and waited for Sunshine to slowly make her way to the dirt road. "My, my, you are really pregnant. My wife, when she was this pregnant with our second son, never left the house, and here you are hiking up and down mountains. Incredible. Just incredible."

"Thank you, Karim," Sunshine said as he helped

her into the front seat of the car. "Your wife is the smart one, that's for sure."

"Yes, I know. You are taking big risks just to leave a place where you so badly wanted to be just a year or so ago."

"Things have changed, Karim. Like I told you on the phone, I wouldn't be doing this unless I had to. The fact that you're helping me, even though you don't have to, means we are friends for life."

"Okay, friend to friend, we have to leave now. Right now."

"You think they followed me here?" Sunshine asked in a voice full of fear.

"No, but I don't want to be late for work. You know how long a drive it is to the airport. I also have you booked on the first flight out. Do you have your passport?"

"Yes, I was able to find it, thank goodness."

"Good. That makes what we are about to do a lot easier, and legal."

"Karim, the last thing I want is for you to get in any trouble."

"It's no trouble at all. Consider it my wedding present."

"But you already gave us a gift at the reception."

"Yes, but my wife picked that out. This is from me to you."

"I'm glad you said that because I have a gift for you, too." Sunshine handed Karim a pouch filled with jewelry and Moroccan money. "Before you say anything, I want you to know this is for you and your family for all you have done for me. Take it and know it means more to me to be able to repay you than the value of the gift."

Karim put the pouch in his glovebox and the two began talking about the next part of the plan, to get Sunshine on a flight to Madrid without drawing any undue attention on her—or the fact she was a very pregnant American fleeing the country to escape a prominent Moroccan family.

With Karim's help, Sunshine had no trouble getting aboard the flight to Madrid. As she sat on the plane, she began to feel the guilt from what she'd done. Salah and his family weren't bad people, they just had very strong beliefs that were different from her own. Setting their house on fire was no way to repay them for all they did for her—helping with the wedding, and giving her a good home for over a year. They had even offered to let Shawn come over and live with them, but he preferred to stay in Acapulco with his school friends and his new band, Peace and Love. Then there was Salah. How would he react to her elaborate escape? She decided the first thing she would do when she arrived safely in Spain was to call him and explain everything. He was in Athens on business, but she could always get hold of him through his office. She knew this was the right thing to do for the baby, but she also wanted to make it right with her husband—and the father of their soon-to-be-born son.

Her husband was mad at first, but quickly calmed down. "Sunshine, I understand. It's okay," Salah said. "One of the reasons I love you is that you are different from the women in my country and culture. The important thing is that you and the baby are safe."

"Oh Salah, I am so glad you aren't mad. I'm so sorry I caused so much trouble for you and your family."

"Sofian called me and told me what happened. Nobody was hurt and the fire only damaged the kitchen."

"I bet your brother is really mad at me."

"Yes he is, but he'll get over it. They all will. What we need to focus on now is to get you somewhere safe where you can have our baby."

"You're going to help me get to America?"

"Of course. I'll come and see you as soon as I can, but until then I want you to be as comfortable as possible."

"But honey, I have no money."

"Tell me where you plan to go and I'll arrange everything. And Sunshine, don't worry, everything is going to be okay."

Salah arranged for a first-class ticket to New York. Sunshine had a hard time getting on the plane because she was eight months pregnant, but she told the woman at the ticket counter her entire story and the airline employee let her get on despite the rules. She said she would want someone to do the same for her if she was ever in the same situation—which she acknowledged she would probably never be.

Once in New York, Salah arranged for an international nanny to help Sunshine with the last month of her pregnancy and remain after the baby was born. The two women stayed in a suite at the Hilton Hotel in New York City with everything taken care of for them by Salah. He called every day to check on them and he planned to be there for the birth.

While visiting friends in New Jersey, Sunshine went into labor and delivered a 10-pound, 2-ounce baby boy she named Kirit, which means, "Crown of the King." Salah changed his plans and booked a private plane to fly from Agadir to Madrid, and then on to New York to see his wife and son. Sunshine was eager to share the joy of their beautiful boy and reunite with her husband in America.

The next morning, Sunshine was awakened by the phone. It was Sofian on the other end. "You have to come back to Morocco," Sofian said, pain in his voice.

"Why would I do that? So you can kidnap my baby and raise him your way. I don't think so," Sunshine said, feeling a twinge of guilt for the harshness of her reply and the fact she set fire to Sofian's family home.

"It's about Salah," Sofian said somberly.

"Salah gave his blessing for Kirit to be born in America. In fact, he is on his way to New York to meet his new son as we speak."

"That's why I called, Sunshine. He's not coming."

Sunshine was so used to doing battle with Salah's younger, more Muslim brother that she couldn't help herself when she said, "So you think you've convinced Salah that I am not worthy of his love. Not worthy to be his bride and the mother to his son. I'm here to tell you that Salah calls me every day and our bond is stronger than you think. He is coming here and if I have my way, he may not be coming back."

Sofian didn't say anything, but didn't hang up, either. After a long pause, he finally said, "Sunshine, Salah is dead. His plane crashed in the Atlas Mountains just after takeoff. He's gone. My brother is gone."

Sunshine was speechless. She didn't know what to

say. Could it be true, or was it a trick to get her to come back? Was it possible she was widowed twice before the age of 35, and both times just after having a baby? No, it couldn't be. It just couldn't. Sunshine said goodbye to Sofian, knowing that if Salah truly was gone, it would be the last time the two spoke to one another.

Still in shock, Sunshine called the Agadir Airport and asked for Karim. Surely, he would tell her that no plane crashed and that this was all a ploy by the family to get her to come back to Morocco so they could steal her baby.

To her horror, Karim confirmed that a private plane crashed and that there were no survivors.

DEAR DIARY *After learning that Salah was killed on his way to see the baby and me, I was filled with so much guilt. It was a very dark time. I did go back to Morocco for the funeral, but I left the baby in New York with the nanny. I really did fear that Kirit would be kidnapped and made to stay there to be raised as a Muslim if I took him with me. The family didn't speak to me at the service, and I don't blame them. I'm not sure if there was a will and if I was in it, and I couldn't care less. I wouldn't have accepted anything even if it was offered. The whole thing felt like it was my fault.*

One thing I did at the time that I wished I had done soon-

er is purchase a camera. I bought a Polaroid instant camera and I became obsessed with capturing every memorable moment — I didn't want to miss a thing. Life truly is too short. I realized I had very few photos of Salah, the palace, my sacred pond, or my friends Omar and Karim. Since then I've taken hundreds of photos with that camera, many times taking two photos with the same person so I could give them a copy and keep one for myself. Pictures are permanent reminders of a moment in time and looking at them can be a very powerful and emotional experience.

1978

HAPPY CAMPER

FORTY YEARS OLD

What do you do when you turn forty, have two kids in tow, and are recently divorced? If you're Sunshine Blake, you buy a VW camper van and travel around Europe. As she would often say, "Travel is the one thing you buy that makes you richer."

After being widowed, Sunshine met and married an aerospace engineer (who also dabbled in real estate) and the two had a whirlwind romance that took them all over the world—including, interestingly enough, Saudi Arabia.

However, she missed her children and wanted to spend more time with them—her sons were both enrolled in a Montessori School in Mexico.

The relationship didn't last long and Sunshine left her third husband, Clyde William Moczygemba, to begin a new chapter of her life.

After the divorce, Sunshine purchased a brand new, fully-loaded Volkswagen Westfalia in Germany that would end up being her home (and a school bus) for years to come as she explored lands near and far—often with her sons. This beige beauty had many of the amenities of a home, only a lot smaller. The pop-top, double-side doors, and many windows made the vehicle look and feel larger than it really was. Inside there was a cozy bed (it served dual purpose), a small fridge and galley, and homey touches like lamps, drapes, and tablecloths. The most important part of her new home away from home was that it was on wheels and could go wherever she wanted, whenever she wanted. It represented freedom.

This chapter is about a few of Sunshine's many adventures while on the road and living in her van—and the life lessons she learned along the way—which she taught to her two sons. This was not just a phase of her life, it was also a way of life that she would fully embrace. Sunshine often referred to herself as a hippie—long after being a hippie was hip—and being a nomad was a big part of her identity as she spread happiness and joy wherever she went.

An Attitude of Gratitude

"Mom, how will Santa know where I am to give me my presents on Christmas?" A young Kirit asked his mom from the back of the van as they drove toward Venice, Italy for the holidays.

"Don't worry, Kirit, Santa knows what you want and where you are," Kirit's big brother Shawn said from the front seat, trying to be helpful.

"What do you want for Christmas, Kirit?" Sunshine wanted to know.

Kirit listed several things, many of them expensive.

"You know, Kirit, today is a gift, that's why we call it the present. Happiness is not something you can buy and it's not something that you put off for the future. It's something you experience in the moment. Like now."

Kirit looked confused, so Shawn jumped in, having heard this before. "What mom is trying to say is even if Santa doesn't bring you any gifts this year, just be happy you're here."

Again, Kirit was unsure what this meant for the prospect of presents finding him in this foreign land.

"Shawn is right. We're all together this year. We're all healthy. And we're traveling around Italy. I think we're all pretty lucky, don't you?" Sunshine chirped.

Shawn jumped in again. "Mom, it would be nice if

we could take a hot shower, cook a real meal, and use a proper bathroom on this trip. I mean, it's fun to see the sights and all, but we're really roughing it here."

"Honey, I know it's not the Taj Mahal—which I've been to by the way—but things could be worse. Someone once said, 'Don't wish things were easier, wish you were better.' There has to be bad times to appreciate the good times, and having you both here with me is what I would call the good times. I miss you two when you're away at school, so let's celebrate our time together this summer."

"Does this mean I won't get any presents?" Kirit asked.

Shawn answered, "That's exactly what it means."

Thumbs Up

Sunshine slowed her van to a stop along a two lane road in rural Germany when she came upon a long-haired man with a green duffle bag slung over his Army jacket, limping alongside the empty tree-lined road in the pouring rain.

"Do you want a ride?" Sunshine asked with a smile. This is not something she would have done if her kids were with her, but since she was on her way to pick them up from a friend's house, she took a chance.

"I'm fine, thanks," the scruffy man said without

making eye contact.

"How about a sandwich, then? I made it myself." Sunshine asked cheerily.

"Thanks, but I'm okay," the American said, still with his head down.

"You're soaking wet, you know," Sunshine said.

"Yeah, I know," the man said, still looking at the ground.

"So why don't you hop in and dry off? We Americans need to stick together, right?" Sunshine asked, pointing out they were from the same country but both now outsiders inside foreign lands.

"I don't accept charity," the man said, finally looking up at her.

"Okay, you can give me some money for gas and we'll call it even. There should be a gas station in the next town, and I always fill up when I can."

"Look, this rain is nothing compared to what I sat in for hours on end in Vietnam. I'll be fine."

Sunshine was about to drive away, but instead she asked the tall stranger, "Okay, can I take your picture then?"

This caught the man by surprise. "Why on earth would you want to take my picture?"

"Because you're a hero. You don't meet many heroes anymore."

"Fine, you can take my picture, but I'm no hero."

"Great, but my camera can't get wet so you'll have to hop in."

With the man's unruly beard, it looked like maybe he was smiling, but Sunshine couldn't be sure. She reached over and popped open the passenger door and the stranger semi-reluctantly, and very slowly, pulled himself up and into the van and said, "Satisfied?"

"Are you?"

"Seriously, what is your deal, lady?"

"No deal, I like helping people and you looked like you could use some help. What's wrong with that?" Sunshine asked while handing him the sandwich she promised. She put the van in gear and started to drive down the deserted road.

"What about that picture?"

"Why don't you dry off and finish your sandwich first?"

The man seated next to her handed Sunshine a five-dollar bill, which she accepted. "You still carry American dollars with you?" she asked.

"That's how Uncle Sam pays me, so yes."

"I'm Barbara, but everyone calls me Sunshine."

"I'm Jeff, and everyone calls me Jeff, or Sarge, I guess."

"Where're you from?" Sunshine asked.

"I'm from a small town in New Jersey."

"Wow, I spent a lot of time in the Garden State. Which town?"

"Nobody's ever heard of it."

"Try me," Sunshine persisted.

"I'm from Westwood. I haven't been back in years. My parents are still there, but I've been wandering around Europe seeing the sights since I was discharged from Landstuhl. It's a military hospital in Germany."

"What happened to you?" Sunshine wanted to know.

"I'd rather not talk about it," Jeff said before taking a big bite of his sandwich so he didn't have to speak.

"Hey, there's a town coming up. Want to get a bite to eat?"

"I'm eating a sandwich," Jeff said with a semi-full mouth.

"Yeah, but now *I'm* hungry," Sunshine said with a smile.

"If I say 'no' you'll just go there anyway, am I right?"

"See, you know me already, Jeff."

The two strangers sat opposite each other in a back booth in a tiny tavern in the town of Rothenburg. It featured dark wood, dark decor, and even darker lighting, but the food smelled delicious.

"So what's your story, Sunshine? Are you one of those Holy Rollers who are trying to save souls? Because if you are, I'm not interested. After what I saw in the jungles of Vietnam, I don't believe in God."

"Jeff, look at me. I'm not asking for anything. I'm not religious, but I do believe in karma—you know, what goes around comes around. Do onto others as you would have them do unto you. You get what you give. If you let people know how much you care about them, they will take care of you. So, whenever I can, I try to help people. I try to be kind to everyone. I'm trying to make the world a better place because I am in it. I want to make a difference in other people's lives. So I am on a crusade of sorts, it's just a personal one."

"And how is that working for you?"

Sunshine pointed to her van in the parking lot and said, "I love that van, but sometimes it doesn't love me back. I've been broken down in the darnedest places, and thanks to the kindness of strangers, I've never had to pay for any repairs—and there's been a ton of 'em."

"Is that why you stopped to give me a ride?"

"No, the van is running fine. You just looked like you were struggling with your leg, and I knew by looking at the map in my lap that the next town was more than just a few miles away, plus it was raining."

"I do fine, even with this bum leg."

"I find it inspiring when people with a condition don't complain."

"It's more than just a condition, Sunshine. I lost my left leg when a mortar round exploded in the foxhole I was in with two other soldiers, both of whom were under my command, and both of whom died. I was checking on them because the attack was their first experience of being under fire. When we heard the shell whistling toward us, I started to duck, but one of my guys pushed me down and then jumped on top of me. He gave up his life so I could live. It haunts me every single day and makes me question why?"

"Why what?"

"Why he had to die so I could live—and for what?"

Sunshine sat silently, not sure what to say. So she simply said, "I wish there was something I could do or say, but I can't think of anything, so instead I want to offer you a smile, if that's okay?"

Jeff stared at Sunshine, tears streaming down his checks, and he opened up about what had happened to him the past four years. Not only had he lost his leg, but his wife and daughter were killed in a car crash while he was recovering from his injuries in an Army hospital. At the time, he was feeling sorry for himself after being wounded in action. He didn't want them to see him as he was maimed and broken, so he stopped writing and stopped caring. If he had only gone home after he was discharged, maybe the loves of his life—his beautiful wife and young daughter—would still be alive, or so he believed. Jeff had lost his will to live and let himself go as he wandered around Europe like a zombie. He drank too much, did whatever drugs he could get his hands on, and he rarely stayed in one place long enough to get to know anyone. With his scraggly appearance, nobody ever talked to him, or even acknowledged him. He told her she was the only person who made him feel like someone cared.

"I never judge people because you don't know their story. You haven't walked in their moccasins, so you can't possibly know what's what. Instead, I honor them as human beings who deserve to be treated with dignity and respect."

"Thank you, Sunshine. I will repay you for your kindness the only way I can, with a smile. It's all I can offer. I hope it's enough."

"Jeff, it's more than enough."

Lost and Found

The narrow winding road was seemingly carved out of the side of the mountain and designed with no regard for driver safety. One wrong turn and a person could plummet to her death on the rocky shoreline a hundred feet below.

It was a struggle for Sunshine to keep her eyes on the road with magnificent views waiting around every corner, but her passengers were counting on her to stay in control of the van as the boys and Sunshine made their way to a small seaside village at the end of the road.

This was not a typical Irish tourist town, which is why Sunshine sought it out. She wanted to show her sons what life was like in a tiny town where hard work was a necessity and sweat equity was a commodity. Sunshine knew what it was like to grow up in a place like this, and she hoped to spend some time here with the boys to give them a lesson in village life. It was her experience that living in a small town teaches people to care and share. If someone was sick, you would bring them soup and help with their chores. If someone was suffering, you offered your support. If someone was successful, you shared in their success and they shared it with you.

Because of her background, Sunshine believed it was better to grow up poor. Her thinking was, if you had very little you appreciated those things a lot more. If you've had everything you ever wanted, and even excess, it is hard to appreciate the little things that make most people happy. Plus, if you were handed something for free, you missed out on the satisfaction of earning it—which in Sunshine's mind was the greatest feeling in the world—except possibly helping others get what they need, which as feelings go, is as good as it gets.

In her extensive travels, Sunshine was constantly curious about what made people happy, so she made it a point to find the time to watch the sunrise and the sunsets wherever she went. It was at these times she would talk to people and ask them about what brings them joy and inner peace. What she found surprised her. Wealthy people weren't any happier than those with almost nothing. In fact, she discovered that some of the poorest people were better off in many ways.

With her funds running low, a working summer vacation was the only way they could continue on their journey, so all three of them would have to find work—which was not easy for an American living abroad. Sunshine hoped they would be accepted into the community and offered jobs. Anything that paid would do at this point.

With her mind on making a good impression on the locals, Sunshine wasn't paying attention to the task at hand—driving—which is why when she suddenly saw the object lying in the road, she swerved to the left and the van almost went flying off the cliff. Fortunately, they were nearly at the base of the mountain and nobody was nearby when she braked in the middle of the road. Slowly, Sunshine put the van in gear, and with her hands shaking, carefully pulled into a cutout on the side of road so other cars could safely pass her.

"What was that thing in the road, Mom?" Kirit asked.

"I don't know, but it was green, wasn't it?" Sunshine asked back.

"It was green, and I know what it is!" Shawn exclaimed.

"What is it?" Sunshine and Kirit said in unison.

"If I'm right, we're going to be okay. Better than okay. We're gonna be rich," Shawn said as he opened the van door to get out.

"Where are you going?" Sunshine asked him.

"You'll see. Stay here, I'll be right back," Shawn said and leapt from the van and made his way back up the road to find the mystery object.

Kirit slid the side door to follow his brother, but Sunshine insisted he stay put while she got out to make sure Shawn was safe.

Shawn ran back down the road toward the van waving something over his head and singing, "We're in the money, we're in the money."

Kirit pushed past Sunshine and started dancing in the street, too, only he wasn't sure why.

"What did you find?" Sunshine asked Shawn.

"A bag full of money. Look," Shawn said and passed her the green bank deposit bag with a lock at the end of a heavy-duty zipper. "It's not locked, it just looks like it is. Go ahead, open it."

Sunshine slowly unzipped the bag that looked like it had been run over a dozen times and sure enough, it was full of cash—lots of it.

Kirit excitedly said, "Count it Mom."

Sunshine zipped the bag back up and inspected it more closely. The bank's name was embroidered in yellow stitching, along with some numbers. There was also a leather name holder sewn into the side of the bag with a see-through window, but the card inside it was blank.

Boy, they sure could use this money. It was enough to keep them going for months, or years even. Maybe it was there as payback for all the good deeds she'd done. Maybe it was from a bank robbery gone bad. Maybe it was just meant to be. Sunshine turned the bag over in her hands a few times and she knew what she would do—

she would do the right thing. It was a chance to teach the boys a valuable lesson about right and wrong, and the importance of being honest and honorable. She believed in being trusting and trustworthy.

"Boys, this money doesn't belong to us. We're going to go into town and turn it in."

"Turn it in? Turn it in to who?" Shawn asked dejectedly.

"It's to whom, and I don't know, yet. Let's go into town, find a place to eat, and see what happens. Maybe someone will mention losing all this money."

"Are we at least gonna spend some on a nice place to stay? I'm really tired of camping out," Kirit said. Not as attached to the money as his brother, but very interested in spending some of it for a good night's sleep.

"No, we aren't going to spend any of it. We also aren't going to tell anyone we have it. If there is a police station, we can turn it in there. If not, well, I have an idea how we can find the rightful owner."

"Where in the world are we going to find the one person who lost all this money?" Shawn wanted to know.

"One of two places," Sunshine replied. "We'll find the person who this bag belongs to either in the church or the pub."

"Mom, I don't want to go to church," Kirit pleaded.

"Neither do I, so hopefully the pub is the place."

The minute they pulled into the sleepy little village, they were in love with it. The charming town was nestled into a valley between two big green mountains, and fronting the waterfront there was a small marina and several quaint shops. They drove through the tiny town and saw a bakery, butcher shop, fish market, and post office, but no bank and no Police station. What they did discover, conveniently located side-by-side, were the town's tavern and only church. Most of the homes were nestled into the hills, while some were closer to town. The old inn was ironically called, The Old Inn, and it was situated right on the road that led to the sea.

Sunshine and her sons pulled up to The Old Inn, which looked like it had been there a long, long time, and went inside where an even older couple greeted them.

"We're looking for a room," Sunshine said as she approached the front desk.

"Well, you've come to the right place. All we have are rooms. How long will you be staying with us?" The elderly innkeeper asked, hunched over the counter with his spectacles down to the edge of his long skinny nose. His shirt and sweater were hanging from his thin frame, and his bald head was covered by a few grey hairs combed over.

"How long we can stay depends on how much the rooms cost," Sunshine said.

"Ah, you're a smart one. What do you think a fair price would be young man?" the innkeeper asked Shawn.

"Free!" he blurted out.

"Okay, free it is," the old man said with a smile.

"Uh-uh. We always pay our way," Sunshine said.

"Good," the wife of the old man replied, "because free don't pay the rent."

"Don't listen to her. We've owned this place outright since the war. But we'll gladly take your money, if you're offering and all."

"It's not our money," Kirit said, not realizing what he was revealing.

Sunshine jumped in while Shawn guided Kirit outside. "Kids," she said. "They say the strangest things."

"Well as long as you're not bank robbers, you're welcome to stay here as long as you'd like."

"Just out of curiosity," Sunshine said, "are there many bank robberies here?"

The couple looked at each other and laughed. "We never had a bank robbery in this town—because there isn't a bank here. If we need to make a deposit or withdrawal, we have to drive back up the road you came in on and clear to the other side of the mountain, because the closest bank is back in the city."

"Well, I feel a lot safer knowing that," Sunshine said, relieved.

"We've got you and your children in room number one. It's down the hall, first door on your left. Here's your key."

Sunshine stared at the key and then asked, "You don't happen to have a safe here at the inn, do you?"

"Why, you planning to rob it?" the innkeeper said with a raised eyebrow and a crooked smile which let Sunshine know he was kidding.

As soon as Sunshine and the boys entered the town's tavern everyone inside turned around to take a look. The bartender was the first to speak. "Welcome strangers. We heard you made your way to our small town today. Hey, everyone, they don't look like bank robbers, do they?"

Everyone in the bar looked at Sunshine and her sons and started laughing.

"Very funny. We are not bank robbers, far from it. We believe in an honest day's work for an honest dollar."

"In that case, how about a beer? And for the little guys, how about something to eat?"

"Thanks, that would be wonderful."

"Can we play darts, too?" Shawn asked.

"Why certainly. Here's a set of darts you can use, but be careful," the friendly bartender said while winking at Sunshine. "They'll be fine," he said to reassure her and passed her a pint.

Sunshine took a sip. She wasn't a big drinker, but by looking around at how many people were in the establishment in the early afternoon, she could tell the patrons could put a few back, so she decided to drink the entire dark beer.

"So, just passing through, or are you on the run?" The man seated on the barstool next to her asked. He looked like a farmer, and smelled like one, too.

"Actually, we'd like to stay a while. I'd love it if the kids could get jobs and learn the value of hard work."

"Good on ya," the man said and slammed his beer back leaving a foam mustache on his face. "My kids have worked every day of their lives. Living on a farm everyone is up at dawn and working until the work is done—especially when it's planting or harvesting time. My kids now live in the city, but they took that strong work ethic with them. Oddly enough, both are in banking." All of a sudden, and after saying the word "banking," the man hung his head and put his face in his hands.

"Are you okay?" Sunshine asked.

"Not really. Have you ever let a whole town down?" the man wanted to know.

Sunshine was about to answer when a much younger man made his way to the bar. He simply nodded to the bartender and a whiskey appeared a moment later. "This is a good man here with good kids. His boys work all day in a bank but at night they play in a band, and they are really good. The girls love 'em." Clearly the younger man was trying to cheer up the older man seated next to her.

"So they do, so they do. A toast to my boys, David and Michael, may they make a fortune in music." Everyone in the bar raised their glasses and said, "aye" and then took a swig. "Secretly, I hope they don't quit their day jobs to pursue the music thing, but I'll support them either way."

"I'm sorry," the young man said, "Let me introduce myself, I'm Ian, and this here is Jackie."

"Nice to meet you both. I'm Sunshine. If you don't mind me asking, what line of work are you in, Ian?"

"I'm the pastor," he replied as if it were perfectly normal to be served a pint in a bar in the middle of the afternoon while serving God. "I know what you're thinking, a man of the cloth drinking in the afternoon seems strange—especially to an American, but here, it's how I keep track of what's happening in the lives of my people."

"Can I talk to you privately?" Sunshine asked the pastor.

"Sure. Let's go sit by your boys. They look like they are enjoying their sandwiches." The two grabbed their drinks and went to a booth in the back.

"I'm not a religious person," Sunshine said, "but I need to talk to someone I can trust."

"Sure, I can take your confession in the back of a bar. I do it all the time."

"Well, it's not really a confession. On second thought, I guess it is."

"Feel free to unburden yourself of anything you want. I'm here to listen and not judge, and if I can help, I'm here for that, too."

"Thank you. Okay," Sunshine said as she exhaled heavily. "On our way into town today we found a bag full of money."

"Was it a green bag, and looked like it came from a bank?" Ian asked, leaning forward in his chair and rubbing his hands together.

"How did you know?"

"Because it's a miracle from God!" Ian said, then asked. "Do you have this bag with you?"

"Uh, yeah. It's in my purse. It seemed like the best place to put it since there's no safe at the Inn"

"Is that your purse?" the pastor asked as he pointed to a shoulder bag on the floor beside Sunshine.

"It is," Sunshine said as she subconsciously reached down and pulled it into her lap. Something in Ian's eyes made her nervous. He was a little too excited about the bag.

"May I see this money bag?" he asked.

Sunshine decided to take her own advice and trust the man with the money. She handed over the bulging bag and watched the pastor's face light up like nothing she'd ever seen before. He examined the bag closely and then looked at her and asked, "Do you know what this means? Do you have any idea what you've done?"

Suddenly feeling sick to her stomach and wondering if the pastor mistakenly thought she was making a donation to the church instead of finding out who the bag belonged to simply said, "No. What does it mean?"

"It means everything. It means there is a God."

"You doubted that?"

"Of course not, but many in this town did. You see, this money belongs to us, all of us. Once a month Jackie rides his motorcycle into the city to see his kids. Since his boys both work in a bank, we give Jackie our money to be deposited. Last week we had a rather large amount of cash that we needed Jackie to deliver. We had a fishing fleet in town that needed supplies, and a place to spend their money, so we all obliged… and prospered.

When Jackie arrived at the bank, the money was gone. He assumed it was stolen when he stopped for a bite to eat (and a drink too, most likely) and left his bike unattended with the money unlocked in a saddlebag on the side. You see, living in a small village your whole life you learn to trust people. You don't lock your doors and you certainly don't expect someone to steal your stuff.

We all forgave Jackie, but he hasn't yet forgiven himself."

Sunshine couldn't help but smile hearing the story. As usual, things always have a way of working out. "Shouldn't you make an announcement or something?" Sunshine asked.

"Right you are." Standing on his chair, the pastor clinked a spoon against a glass. "Everyone! Can I have your attention? Is anyone missing a dark green bank bag?"

"That's cruel," someone said.

Ian ignored him and said, "Because this fine woman and her two sons just handed me this bag full of money she found on the side of the road." With that, he held it up high for all to see and the place went berserk. Some cheered, some rushed over to Jackie to pat him on the back, others ran outside to spread the word, and the bartender shouted, "Drinks are on the house!"

The one thing everyone did was to come over and personally thank Sunshine, Shawn, and Kirit for their honesty and integrity. Jackie walked over and hugged them all with tears in his eyes. It had been a hard few days while the money was missing. The people in the town were not happy about what happened, but they never blamed him—although he blamed himself. Throughout the day, the people from the town made their way to the pub to meet this fine family and offer them everything from free food to free lodging (courtesy of the owners of The Old Inn). The town also insisted Sunshine accept a cash reward for finding the lost money. She reluctantly accepted it, explaining that doing the right thing was reward enough, but she was broke. She split the money with Shawn and Kirit, making them responsible for their share. She had them spend it on the things they wanted and to get a better sense of how much things cost.

Sunshine and the boys lived in the village longer than anywhere else they had stayed on their extensive road trip, and they all worked at various jobs for both the experience and to pull their own weight. It was a wonderful time, and when they finally left in their van to head out for their next adventure, Shawn said, "Mom, please keep your eyes on the road—you never know what you may find."

DEAR DIARY *A house on wheels was the best thing for me. I'm a gypsy at heart and I don't like to stay in one place too long. I owned that van for 20 years and had it shipped to the United States. I drove that thing everywhere, and often lived in it. I bet it would still be going strong, if it wasn't totaled in a head-on collision—which is a story for another day.*

I exchanged addresses with Jeff, the Vietnam veteran I met in Germany. He gave me his parent's home address, figuring he would eventually end up back there someday, and he did. We became pen pals after he pulled his life together, and went on to compete in the Paralympics and became an inspiration to others with his positive attitude. He even became a motivational speaker (which seemed strange based on how bitter and shy he was when we first met). He spoke about the power of positive thinking and that life boils down to your attitude. It doesn't matter what happens to you, it's how you handle it. He would always say, if people have the time to complain about something, then they also have the time to do something about it.

When it came to finding the money bag, I knew it was the perfect opportunity to teach my sons a valuable lesson about doing the right thing. I can honestly say what they learned from finding the rightful owners of that money and giving it back was far more valuable than the money itself.

When the kids were with me, it was like they were experiencing the things they would have only read about in school. We visited museums, experienced local cultures, and hiked and swam in the most beautiful of places. With everything that went wrong along the way, I think it taught the kids how to have a sense of humor about those things that are out of our control and go wrong. We also met the most interesting people along the way—others traveling in vans would always stop to talk and offer to help, and people from other parts of the world were very curious about our western ways. Maybe the most important lesson of all is to be flexible and spontaneous—and that you can never truly be lost. Some of the most amazing sights we saw were things we stumbled upon when we were "lost." It was the out-of-the-way and off-the-beaten-path places that turned out to be the best.

1987

NASHVILLE OR BUST

FORTY-NINE YEARS OLD

When you live your life like a country western song (heartbreak, tragedy, wanderlust, and love), eventually you may end up in one—which is what happened to Sunshine after she made her way to Nashville, Tennessee.

If a person was planning to spend some time in Nashville, they would likely want to be where all the action is, and that place in 1987 was the Grand Ole Opry Hotel. The hotel was where the stars stayed (and partied) when appearing at the famous venue located right next door. The popular television show, *Hee Haw* was also taped there.

If you guessed Sunshine both lived at the Grand Ole Opry Hotel and appeared on *Hee Haw*, you would be correct. The success of the show had a lot to do with the popularity of Buck Owens and Roy Clark, the hosts, as well as the regular cast members (most of them famous in their own right) and the many musical acts who appeared as guests. However, a good many male viewers tuned in to see the show's scantily clad women who had bit parts and sang backup during the many skits. Sunshine was one of those women.

"Are you one of the showcase artists?" Sunshine asked the very un-country-music-like-looking man standing next to her watching the crew set the stage for the next skit. He stood there wearing flip-flops, shorts, and a t-shirt that read, "Bite me."

"No, I'm here to *report* on one of the showcase artists," the man with the long hair and bushy mustache said as he held up his pen and pad of paper to prove he was indeed a writer.

"Are you a music reviewer?" Sunshine wanted to know, stepping aside as a crew member passed with the cue cards for the next bit.

"No, I report on the Nashville scene for a music magazine."

Sunshine pondered that and said, "But you really want to make it in the music business as a performer, not a reporter, am I right?"

"Of course. Doesn't everyone in Nashville want a record deal? "

"Not me," Sunshine stated.

"Why not?"

"I don't want to be a star. I'd rather help others reach their goals. I'm more like a cheerleader on the sidelines than a player on the field," Sunshine said.

This struck the young wanna-be recording artist/reporter as odd so he pulled his pen from behind his ear and asked, "What's your name?"

"Sunshine. I'm one of the newest members of the 'Hee Haw Honeys.'"

"I can see that," the reporter said trying not to stare too much at Sunshine's stunning good looks. "I'm Jimmy. Tell me, Sunshine, what's it like to be on the show?"

"There's a lot of singing, dancing, and a little acting—but we don't have to memorize our lines because, as you could probably tell, they're on cue cards. Mostly, it's a lot of standing around, like now," Sunshine said while waving at someone across the soundstage.

"So you're a singer?" Jimmy wanted to know.

"I'm working on it. Mostly the girls and I are the backup singers for the show."

"How did you get the job if you're not a real singer?" Jimmy asked, actually writing down her answers.

"Well, when the producer who interviewed me asked if I could sing, I told him the same thing I told you, that I was working on it. I could see he was skeptical, so I said I believe success is 90 percent hard work and 10 percent talent. If you're not good at something, work harder. The harder you work, the more talented you become. The producer liked that and hired me without an audition— thank goodness. But I am getting better."

"Do you really believe success is more about hard work than talent?"

"Of course I do, or I wouldn't have said it."

"Sorry. Of course."

The awkwardness was interrupted when some of the cast members walked by on their way to tape their skit, the iconic barn backdrop now finished being erected on stage.

"Hey there Archie, Junior, Grandpa," Sunshine said as they walked past.

"Hey there yourself, Sunshine," Grandpa Jones said.

Misty Rowe walked by and said, "Hey Sunshine, the girls are all gonna go to Tootsie's or Fran's later, wanna come? You can bring your friend," Misty added with a wink, making Jimmy blush. After she was a few steps closer to the stage she turned around and asked, "You ready for your first 'Amateur Minute' performance, Sunshine?"

"It's not like I need to practice singing off key," Sunshine said to Misty.

"Sure you can," Misty said loudly. "I do it all the time."

Sunshine laughed and Jimmy asked her, "What was that all about?"

"Oh, it's nothing. All the cast members get a chance to sing or yodel badly and get booed off the stage in a little skit we call 'Amateur Minute.'"

"Interesting."

"You don't watch the show, do you Jimmy? Shame on you."

"I listen to so much country music in my line of work, when I get home I just wanna grab a beer, put my feet up, and watch something funny."

"You should tune in sometime. It's not a country music show, it's a comedy show with country music in it."

"Was Misty serious about going to Tootsie's? There's a lot of music history in that place. Did you know that Willie Nelson got his first songwriting gig after performing there?" Jimmy announced.

"I did not know that. Maybe you should play there, Jimmy."

Avoiding the suggestion, Jimmy asked, "When will you be done here?"

"This time of year I'm told all the shows are shot at once and then pieced together over the summer and shown later. I still have to do my segment and I think they want to reshoot the 'All-Jug Band' musical sketch we did this morning. Lulu wasn't happy with the way it turned out. Why don't you stick around and we'll go together."

"Sounds good to me. I still have to see how John Schneider performs," Jimmy said, putting his pad back in his back pocket and tucking his pen behind his ear.

"The cute blonde guy from *Dukes of Hazzard*."

"Yeah, but he's here to sing something from his new album."

"I know, I heard him perform. You missed it."

"Dang it. Did I miss Reba, too?" Jimmy asked.

"Nope, she's right over there," Sunshine said pointing to the country star.

"I'm going to go talk to her. I'll come look for you later. It was a pleasure meeting you, Sunshine."

"Same here," Sunshine said, and hustled over to find the other girls.

Jimmy and Sunshine did go to Tootsie's Orchid Lounge together that night and ran into one of Jimmy's friends, another aspiring singer-songwriter with dreams of making it big. Since Jimmy was married, he became a matchmaker for his old and new friend—although the relation-ship got off to a rather rough start.

"I'm Barney Blake, I play country music."

Sunshine reached out to shake his hand. "I'm Sun-shine and I love country music. Where can I hear you play?"

"Well, I, uh, I work days as an aviation expert."

"You mean an airplane mechanic?" Sunshine asked with a knowing smile.

"How did you know?"

"Your hands. You have the hands of a mechanic."

"Yeah, well, I want to be a full-time musician, but I have to pay the bills, you know? For now, I'm working at Berry Field servicing private planes for some of Nash-ville's biggest stars. It's a living."

"Have you thought about changing your name?" Sunshine asked without worrying about his feelings.

"What's wrong with my name?" Barney wanted to know.

"Oh, I don't know. Nothing, I guess. That's not true. Your name should say something about you or who you want to be."

"Is Sunshine your real name?"

"No, see, my real name is Barbara, but it didn't fit."

"So what should I be called, Moonshine?"

"That's not bad, actually—especially for a country music star."

"Well I'm not going to call myself Moonshine. It makes me sound like a hick."

"Okay, what's your middle name then?"

"Luke."

"Hey, what about Luke Blake for your stage name?"

Barney pondered the name for a moment and said, "I like it."

Over the next few months Barney "Luke" Blake and Sunshine became close friends, then lovers, and eventually husband and wife. Barney was head over heels with Sunshine and fascinated with her life story, so much so he wrote a song about her called "International Lady" and went into the studio to record the song as a single.

"Luke, guess what? Ronnie Milsap is recording in the next room. We should go meet him."

"I don't know, Sunshine. I get nervous around celebrities. You're not afraid to approach anyone, anywhere, anytime because you're not afraid to hear the word 'no.' You're fearless, which is one of the things I love about you. Opposites do attract, I guess."

"I love you, too. But I'm not fearless, I'm actually

afraid of missing out on an opportunity and that's why I talk to everyone—famous or not."

"I know. You've been in Nashville less than a year and you know more people than I do, and I've lived here my whole life. You've met Vince Gill, Garth Brooks, and Guy Clark."

"Don't forget Loretta Lynn. Sure, I met them all on the *Hee Haw* set, which made it easier since I was on the show. That's why we should walk over there right now. If ever there was a time to meet someone like Ronnie Milsap, it's today. I mean, you're here recording your song one studio over from him."

"I don't know. I mean look at me—I'm still wearing my work clothes," Barney said, pointing to his name embroidered on his striped and stained blue mechanics jersey.

"It doesn't matter," Sunshine said, squeezing his arm.

"Sure it does," Barney replied. "I don't want him to see me like this."

"Don't worry about it," Sunshine said.

"I am worried about it."

"It's okay, honey. Ronnie Milsap is blind."

"Oh yeah, right," Barney said, finally getting it.

"That's what I love about him. He's making it in

Nashville—a town that chews talented people up and spits them out—and Ronnie is a star who can't see. I find that inspiring, don't you?"

"All I know is I wish I had a hit song like 'How Do I Turn You On?'" Barney said. Looking around the control room of the studio he stopped to stare at a framed poster hanging on the wall next to a large tape machine that read, "The Nashville Sound," which showed Chet Atkins putting new strings on his guitar—the same kind of guitar Barney played, a Gretsch.

"If you want results, you have to take action—and you are, honey. Now let's go find out what's happening in Studio One and see if we can meet Mr. Milsap while we wait for the engineer to get here. What do you say?"

"I say, I love you, my International Lady."

The single, "International Lady," came out in 1987 on the Rustic Records label. Sunshine and her husband roared around Nashville in Barney's bright red Chevy Camaro, complete with a menacing blower protruding through the hood which made the car not only super-fast, but also loud and illegal. The car didn't fit Barney's personality at all, but he spent most of his money and all of his free time working on it to try and gain the respect he relished.

In many ways it worked. Some of the Nashville DJs

were muscle car enthusiasts, so the Camaro was a conversation starter when they saw and heard him pull up. Sunshine couldn't, and wouldn't, put cash and cocaine in a record sleeve to try to gain airtime for a song—which is what professional pitch men did on a regular basis—but the car did open a few doors.

Unfortunately, the song and the marriage didn't make it, but Sunshine enjoyed every minute of her time in Nashville and when it was time to move on, she was ready.

She packed up her van and headed to Las Vegas, somewhere she'd always wanted to go. Her plan was to take her time driving across the country, stopping to see the sights along the way. However, while heading west on Interstate 40, just outside of Amarillo, a driver heading the other way swerved into Sunshine's side of the road and his car collided violently with her van.

DEAR DIARY *It's funny how things work out. The van was a total loss, so I just left it by the side of the road. I decided to hitchhike my way to the nearest airport, but after walking a while on the side of the empty road—and under the blazing hot Texas sun—I was really starting to feel the effects of the crash. I must have passed out because all I remember is looking up at a man so large he blocked out the sun. I said to him, "Am I* *dead?" He just laughed and said, "Not if I can help it," as he got me to my feet.*

I told him I was a damsel in distress and he was my knight in shining armor. Even though the closest airport was a two-hour drive and out of his way, the kind man insisted on driving me there so I could catch a flight from Lubbock to Las Vegas. After a most enjoyable ride and a late lunch, my new friend insisted on making sure I got off okay—and didn't pass out again. When we got to the ticket counter, I ended up being $40.00 short. Without hesitation, he loaned me the money. He gave me his address and I promised to send him the forty bucks as soon as I settled in Nevada.

I did send him a check and we corresponded back and forth for years. In fact, in one of my letters to him many years later I mentioned I was short of breath, which wasn't like me. Jerry called me right away and insisted I see a doctor. I'd never been to a doctor in my life (except when I was pregnant) because I'd never been sick before. I thought that maybe I had a really bad chest cold, but because it was Jerry, and he said he had a bad feeling about this, I took his advice, found a doctor in the Yellow Pages and went in to see what was wrong. It was then (in 2009) that I was diagnosed with a collapsed lung and Stage Four Lung Cancer. Jerry saved my life... twice—which is strange, considering how we met. Again, I don't believe in chance, so it was no accident that Jerry was the one who found me lying by the side of the road. I truly believe it was fate.

While I was in Las Vegas, I met a man named Paul Fisher. He had run for the Democratic Party's Presidential nomination in 1960 against John F. Kennedy. Obviously, he didn't win. It didn't matter because Paul was more famous for inventing a revolutionary ballpoint pen that would work anywhere, including in space. NASA purchased his Fisher Space Pen and it was used on the Apollo missions.

I found the man fascinating, even though he was seventy-five years old when we met — twenty-five years my senior. We connected on a lot of levels. Like me, he was an avid reader and a lifelong learner. I thought his ideas about taxation were brilliant and so was his book, The Plan. Paul became my fifth husband, which seems weird, unless you were there, then you would understand.

1990

BULA, BULA FROM FIJI

FIFTY-TWO YEARS OLD

If there was one thing Sunshine loved as much as experiencing new things, it was sharing those experiences with others through pictures and postcards. No matter where she was in the world or how busy she was, Sunshine always took the time to write to her friends and family. She may have been disconnected by 3,000 miles and three time zones, but Sunshine stayed connected with the people she cared about through the U.S. Mail. Her postcards from this time in her life tell the story of how she ended up working with Anthony Robbins at his exclusive resort in Fiji.

> *"I'm in California and I just met the most amazing person. His name is Tony Robbins. I attended one of the Mastery events he held at his home—it's actually a castle—in Del*

Mar. Wow! He was so inspiring. I walked across burning hot coals that were over 1,000 degrees and no, I didn't burn my feet. I was the first to arrive at the event so I helped with the set-up and I got to meet his wife Becky and their kids. I think I'm going to start working for Tony if there's an opening. This is so me. Talk to you soon."

Sunshine loved the Mastery program so much she signed up for a much longer and intensive week-long event called Date With Destiny. Robbins required total immersion and made the days long and hard, but Sunshine loved every minute of it. She was one of the hearty few who could handle the hours of introspection and insight—while fasting and not getting much sleep. She loved learning about herself and understanding why other people behave the way they do. She was energized by what she was hearing and by how others were reacting. For most attendees, being a part of this experience was life-changing, and that was true for Sunshine, too.

"You have got to come and see Tony. I think I can get you tickets since I'm now one of the crew. I'm a Destiny Dancer, which is just a fancy term for being a cheerleader on stage. It's a lot of clapping and jumping around, but we do have a few routines worked out. I also help people

with the different challenges. You would love it because it feels like a rock concert and a revival all at the same time. It's hard to explain, but the energy in the room is amazing. Everyone is positive and supportive and there's lots of hugging. The best part is I get to work with the man who learned from my personal hero, Jim Rohn. Here's a quote I think you'll like from Jim. 'If you want to harvest in the fall, you must plant in the spring.' I'm planting seeds to see if Tony will send me to Hawaii or Fiji. I'll let you know what happens. Gotta go, fingers crossed."

The challenges attendees faced at the various Anthony Robbins events were designed to push people past their boundaries and get them outside of their comfort zone. To make people feel confident they could do things they didn't think they could required the crew to get everyone pumped up, and nobody was better at leading the charge with chants and cheers than Sunshine. For example, when she was helping people prepare for the fire walk, she would chant, "Yes! Yes! Yes!" and get everyone waiting to go to cheer the others on. When it was their turn she would simply shout, "Eyes up, now go!" and let the adrenaline do the rest.

"To me, a family doesn't mean people have to be related.

I feel like I am part of something special and I consider the other crew members my brothers and sisters. Tony says in life we need either inspiration or desperation to make us do and be more than we think we can. Lately, inspiration is the driving force in my life. I'm so grateful to be able to do the work I'm doing I sometimes have to pinch myself to make sure it's not a dream. I hope you're happy, too."

Behind the scenes, there was so much prep work to get ready for an event that an advance team would often arrive a few days early to make sure everything was in place when the attendees arrived and Tony took the stage. Since Sunshine loved to travel, was a hard worker, and an important part of the crew, she became a key member of the advance team. Sometimes the events were close to home, other times they were in faraway places.

"Aloha. I'm at the Maui Marriott preparing for a Mastery University event. There's so much work to do. Of course we have the fire walk, but we also challenge people to climb up these 40-foot telephone poles and balance on top. Then they have to take a leap of faith and grab a crossbar before we lower them down. I tried it out today and it was so exhilarating. From the top of the pole, I

could see up and down the west Maui coast, islands in the distance, and the beach below. Now that we're all set up I'm heading into town, I hear Kimo's on Front Street has the best views and the freshest fish. We'll be in Los Angeles next. Hopefully, we'll see each other there."

When Sunshine learned Anthony Robbins owned his own resort on a remote island in Fiji, she knew she had to go—and she did.

"I missed you at Date With Destiny in Los Angeles. I think you were there, but it was a big crowd. I was in the back selling books and tapes. (Surprise, surprise, they put me in charge of sales.) I had on a black shirt like the rest of the crew, but I also wore a big smile because I am loving this job. I get to hear Tony over and over again. Sometimes it seems like he is talking directly to me. Just the other day he said, "The only person who is truly holding you back is you. No excuses, it's time to change and live at the next level." That is so true. So, I thought you would want to know, I am leaving for Fiji tomorrow to set up for an event and then I plan to stay on and work at Namale, the resort Tony owns. I can't wait."

People gravitated towards Sunshine because she was always friendly, positive, and a very good listener. One of the reasons she worked with Tony Robbins was the kind of people she came in contact with—people who wanted to better themselves in every way possible, and were committed to the process of making it happen. As the consummate cheerleader, she was always there to support and encourage attendees to push past their fears to improve and grow. She would often tell people, "You are stronger than you know. You can handle and overcome whatever is stopping you from being who you want to be."

It was extremely satisfying to help people break through their barriers, but what gave her the biggest thrill was meeting some of the people Tony talked about and brought in. One person in particular made an impact on her life. His name was W. Mitchell, and he survived two horrific accidents that left him both badly burned and paralyzed. He reaffirmed what Sunshine already knew. If a blazing motorcycle accident and a paralyzing plane crash four years later didn't diminish his determination, what was her excuse? If he could take responsibility for the countless changes and challenges in his life to become a motivational speaker and business leader, how can anyone complain about what's happened in their life?

Most people going to a remote resort on a tropical island would be looking forward to rest and relaxation.

Instead, Sunshine was interested in getting out and meeting the locals in the poorest parts of town, and immersing herself in their way of life, and participating in their rituals.

"I made it. I'm in Fiji. We flew from Nadi to Savusavu on a tiny pontoon plane that reminded me of my magazine sales days. The people I'm traveling with were terrified during the flight, but I loved the adventure of it all. I spotted pilot whales when we were over the ocean, and I saw all kinds of tiny towns (villages) I can't wait to visit when I have the time. You should have seen the airport, it was just a shack in the middle of nowhere. I love it. I'm staying at a hotel near Namale, and right now we are all getting things ready for the Life Mastery event happening later in the week. I did sneak off and explore the grounds of the resort, and it's stunning. There are pools everywhere you turn, private beaches, all kinds of tropical plants, and the whole place looks like it was carved out of wood. I'll tell you more about it in my next postcard."

After a successful event that involved the locals and included a lot of their culture, Sunshine decided she wanted to stay on the island a little longer. Her short stay turned into a long working vacation as she caught on at the exclusive resort—which is known for hosting the rich and famous and boasts a staff of a hundred workers for a maximum of forty-two guests. Most of the employees were Fijians, but many of the guests were from North America, so Sunshine was there not only to make sure the resort was run according to Tony's high standards, but also interact with the English-speaking guests and tend to their needs.

> "Today I ventured along the Hibiscus Highway and visited the home of one of the people I work with here at the resort. She lives across the bay and walks to work every day, so I thought I would give it a try. She also works at the Cousteau Island Resort and I'm going there with her tomorrow. This is a large island and without a car, it's hard to get around, so I am hoping to get a ride to Labasa. It's on the northeastern part of Vanua Levu (the island I'm on) and it's about a two-hour drive from Savusavu. It's a little bit like Lihue, Kauai. It's where most of the locals live and there are schools, a police station, and a post office—which is where I will mail this postcard from. I hope you get it."

Sunshine often explained that her reason for being on Fiji

(or anywhere for that matter) was to help people, set a good example, and be happy. Her belief was that what you put out you get back, so she tried to exude what she craved in return—positive energy. She strived to walk her talk and live in the light instead of being distracted by the dark side—which would have been easy considering some of the things that had happened to her. One of the things that fascinated her most while living in Fiji was the difference between the tourists and the locals. Those who visited the island tended to be people with material wealth, but many were unhappy. By Western standards, the Fijian people were poor, but generally very happy.

One night at the resort a group of tourists got into a long discussion about philosophy with Sunshine and one of her co-workers, a native of the island. An American asked the Fijian what he thought the meaning of life was. Sunshine was not surprised by the man's answer, because it was her belief as well. She watched her co-worker hold back from laughing at the stupidity of the question before he politely replied, "The meaning of life is to be happy, of course. If a person is not happy, it is by choice. Happiness is in our head. Material things do not make us happy. We are all able to experience happiness no matter what we have or don't have." The man who asked the question scoffed at the notion that happiness was not tied to achievement, and explained that where he was from, those who were successful felt better than those who were struggling. The Fijian just shrugged and walked away, smiling as he did so.

> "Bula. That's how you say hello in Fijian. I'm sorry I haven't written to you much lately, but I've been really busy. There's so much to do here. I've ridden a horse on the beach, hiked in a hidden rainforest, swam under a waterfall, and snorkeled the most amazing reef I've ever seen. I've also spent a lot of time exploring the island and getting to know the locals and their culture. Since I've been here all I've worn are traditional Fijian clothes (which are really comfy) and eaten only local dishes (they are delicious and very healthy). The villagers have allowed me to be a part of their spiritual rituals, and I've drank quite a bit of kava—a drink made from the root of a plant. It doesn't taste all that great, but it's an important part of the culture. I miss you and will be back in San Diego soon to work with Tony again—he was just here, by the way."

Sunshine returned to the states and resumed her work with Tony Robbins. Once again her life would change in an unexpected way.

"You won't believe this, but I have a stalker. Okay, that's not quite right. I have a very enthusiastic fan. He is handsome and charming, but he's almost half my age. He insists he's in love with me, but we hardly know each other. He said the minute he saw me on stage as a Destiny Dancer he was determined to meet me and maybe even marry me. Is that crazy, or is it love at first sight? I'm not sure, but he's in sales so his boss sent him to see Tony twice, and both times we had dinner afterward. I'm sure people think I'm with my son when we're together, but I don't care. I'm not concerned what other people think about me. I'm more concerned about what I think of myself. My own truth is what's important, not people's perceptions about me. Hopefully you will get to meet him when we're in San Diego."

Sunshine fell in love with Shaun Browne and they were soon married. They lived in San Diego when they weren't traveling together. His sales job called for him to frequently travel to South America. While he was in Costa Rica he became extremely ill from a rare but deadly virus. He died there from complications due to the disease. He was only forty years old.

DEAR DIARY *I don't think I will ever marry again. When you* *have been widowed four times like I have, you start to wonder if having a husband is healthy—for them. I always say if something doesn't kill you, it makes you stronger. I think I'm strong enough now.*

1998

RUN TO THE VOLCANO

SIXTY YEARS OLD

When Sunshine turned sixty, she made a promise to herself and others that she would do something nobody thought a person her age could do, and she would combine it with a way to give back. She settled on running a marathon—her first—and raising money for cancer research. In addition to training for the 26.2-mile run, Sunshine worked hard to raise thousands of dollars in donations. She'd put her heart and soul into the challenge and was heading to Hawaii to see her goal through when she met a man who would inspire her for years to come.

"That's a beautiful lei. Usually we see people wearing these on their return from Hawaii," the welcoming United Airlines flight attendant said as Sunshine boarded the plane.

"I know. My friends bought this for me somewhere in San Diego."

"You have nice friends."

"Thanks, I know," Sunshine said as the line to board the plane inched forward.

"First time in Hawaii?" the flight attendant asked.

"Yup. It's also my first marathon."

"Good for you," the friendly flight attendant replied.

"No, good for people with cancer," Sunshine said. "I'm running the marathon to raise money for cancer research."

"Are you a cancer survivor?" The flight attendant wanted to know.

"No, but I want to do something for those who have cancer. It's a terrible thing. Plus, I believe that helping others is why we are on the planet in the first place," Sunshine said as the line was now moving into the first-class section of the plane.

"Do you mind stepping out of line for a minute?" the flight attendant politely asked.

"Sure," Sunshine replied.

The two were standing in the area where the flight attendants prepare drinks and store the food carts when she said, "Hi, my name is Jeannie. I lost my mother to cancer last year and I love what you're doing. How would you like to sit in first class?"

"Well, yeah. That sounds great."

"Let me see your ticket," Sunshine handed Jeannie her boarding pass and the flight attendant looked at her name.

"Barbara?" she asked.

"Everyone calls me Sunshine."

"Of course. Well, your middle seat at the back of the plane is now on the aisle up front with me. I'll be serving you and you'll be sitting next to someone I think you'll really hit it off with. Come with me."

The flight attendant led Sunshine forward and when they got to the only open seat in first class Jeannie said, "Wally, this is Sunshine. She's your flying companion for today."

The man took off his Panama hat and flashed the brightest and warmest smile Sunshine had ever seen. "Aloha," he said, tipping his hat toward her lei. "My name is… "

"Wait, I know who you are, you're Famous Amos," Sunshine said and began laughing. "I just bought your book to read on the flight."

"Splendid. Would you like me to sign it?"

"Yes, yes," Sunshine said, and pulled out her copy

of *The Power in You* from her tote bag and handed it to the author.

"Well, aren't you going to sit down?" Wally "Famous" Amos asked.

"Yeah, sorry. I just can't believe it's you."

Wally signed the book using one of the pens he had in the pocket of his aloha shirt and handed it back to her along with a bag of cookies. "What are these for?" Sunshine asked.

"Sweets for the sweet," Wally said and burst out laughing. It was a wonderful, infectious laugh that made her laugh, too.

Sunshine got herself situated and stored her stuff as the crew prepared the plane for takeoff. Jeannie walked over and asked the two if they wanted a quick drink before the plane left the gate. Wally smiled and asked for milk, and Sunshine said, "Make that two."

They both ate a bag of Famous Amos cookies together and drank their milk while others around them enjoyed more tropical (and alcoholic) drinks with umbrellas in them. Sunshine settled in for takeoff and opened her new book to glance at the inscription, which read, "The Power is Love, Wally Amos."

"Are you on vacation?" Sunshine asked Wally Amos as

the plane began to level off for the four-hour flight to Oahu.

"No, no, no, I live here—in Kailua. Keebler just bought my Famous Amos brand and they brought me back to be the spokesman again. So now I'm out traveling around the country making personal appearances again, but I can't wait to get home."

"I didn't even know you weren't a part of the cookie company anymore. I mean, your name's on every bag."

"It's a long story."

"I've got time," Sunshine said with one of her own signature smiles.

"No, I'm always talking about myself, I'd rather hear about you. Are you heading to Hawaii for a vacation?" the cookie icon asked.

"Not really. I'm running in a marathon," Sunshine replied.

"Oh right, the Honolulu Marathon. My friends tell me that the last couple of miles are the toughest because they go up the side of Diamond Head. You know, the volcano."

"I can handle it. With what I've been through in my life, this is nothing."

"I like your style, Sunshine. Tell me something that happened to you in your past that even though it was tough to go through, you're glad you did," Wally wanted to know, and turned in his seat so he could look her in the eyes while he listened to her answer.

"Whew, I don't know where to begin. I guess it was finding out that my parents didn't want me and then sending me to live with relatives who didn't want me either."

"But it made you stronger, right?" Wally said.

"Absolutely," Sunshine replied without hesitation.

"You know how I got the recipe for my cookies?"

"No, I don't."

"After my parents divorced they sent me to live with my aunt Della in New York, and she made the best cookies. So it was my aunt's recipe that I used to develop my own. Funny how it all worked out. I believe good comes from every situation. How about you, Sunshine?"

"If someone looked at my life they would probably see a string of failures, but what I see is a string of lessons learned that made me stronger and better able to help others through tough times, because I've been there, done that."

Wally nodded his head in agreement since he had also been through turbulent times and seen tremendous success. "Did you know that I've never been to college, yet I feel like I have several different degrees from my life experiences?"

"Wow, that's so weird. I didn't go to college either, which in a way was a good thing. I think education is great, but sometimes it can limit a person's thinking, you know what I mean?" Sunshine asked.

"I think I do, but go on."

"I haven't done anything the conventional way, which a lot of times was the only way—I just didn't know any better."

"You know what I believe, Sunshine? I believe that nothing is an obstacle unless you say it is. Look at me, I worked my way up from the mailroom at the William Morris Agency to a talent agent working in a division that didn't even exist before. When I looked around back then, I was the only African-American talent agent there. I took a path that I bet a lot of other people thought was impossible."

Sunshine nodded her head in agreement and said, "I think a lot of people make excuses about why they can't do something. You know what I think? I think they're afraid to fail, or afraid to take a chance of losing what they have to go after what they really want. It's a shame because I believe the universe is sending each person an opportunity to have it all, and all they have to do is act. I'm convinced our life is determined by which opportunities we run with and which ones we don't. The universe gives everyone everything they need, but it's the people who are bold enough to take a chance and go for it who end up having the happiest of lives."

"You know, that's so true. Here's a perfect example of exactly what you're talking about," Wally Amos said in his upbeat voice. "When I was in the service years and years ago I was stationed at Hickam Air Force Base in Honolulu. When I got out I went back to the mainland, and that's where I lived for a long time, but Hawaii was always somewhere I felt I belonged. So in 1977 I came back for four days to sell Famous Amos Cookies and stayed at the Hilton Hawaiian Village. I decided then and there that I would move to Hawaii, and I did. Best decision I ever made."

"It must be a great place to live," Sunshine said.

"It is, but not for the reasons you probably think— and why so many tourists come to visit the islands. You know, the water, weather, and beaches. Those are all nice, but what makes Hawaii special are the locals. You can't out-give the Hawaiian people. You just can't. That spirit of giving is something I have always believed in, even when I lived on the mainland. You can't be a part of the community here until you give back to the community. If you come to Hawaii with an open heart and ask what you can give instead of what you can take, they will be with you forever."

Sunshine pondered Wally's words and said, "I saw an episode of *Star Trek* once where your wealth was determined by how many people you helped instead of how much money you made—the more you gave the more you got. If only that were the way it was in real life, I'd be rich."

"Then you are rich, because nobody is poor if they give back. Of all the things I've accomplished, do you want to know what I am most proud of?"

"I do."

"My work to help end illiteracy in America," Wally proudly stated.

"Do you work with children or adults?" Sunshine asked.

"Sadly, both."

"Well, I know I am looking forward to reading your book. I love what you wrote inside."

"Just remember Sunshine, everything can be resolved when you put love first," and with that, the cookie connoisseur tipped his wide-brimmed hat down and went to sleep.

DEAR DIARY *Out of the blue, I received a postcard from a famous friend who was holding a writing retreat in her beauti-*

ful home in upstate New York. Of course I accepted and made the trip to spend a week in the most amazing Frank Lloyd Wright-inspired home I'd ever seen. The style of the Usonian exterior was stunning in its simplicity and clean lines, and the floor-to-ceiling windows that looked out onto a lake and a forest of tall trees was mesmerizing. The house itself was a work of art, but hanging on the walls throughout the home were rare and valuable pieces of art that had come from a connection to the collection of famous gallery owner Edith Halpert, a mutual friend.

To say I was inspired by my surroundings and the people who surrounded me was an understatement. Although I didn't do much writing during the week, I became committed to writing a book about my life and giving old age a good name. I mean I just completed my first marathon at the age of sixty, so why not make others believe that it's never too late to chase their dreams? I decided I would walk my talk and get busy writing. The first step was to move to an out-of-the-way place in Southern California and focus on finishing my book—or at least get started on it.

2003

FIRE ON THE MOUNTAIN

SIXTY-FIVE YEARS OLD

Sunshine settled into a home near the hills of Ramona, California, a quiet community an hour east of San Diego. Her reason for moving from urban to suburban was to get away from distractions and finally start writing a book—something she'd been talking about doing for years.

Her modest ranch-style home was in a remote portion of the tiny town and backed up to the Cleveland National Forest. Her nearest neighbor to the west maintained a stable of a dozen horses that were lovingly used for riding lessons, equestrian camps, and horseback riding programs for children with special needs. Naturally, Sunshine was a frequent visitor and often volunteered her time to help out with the horses.

Sunshine's lot was large—but her home was small—and her backyard was barren except for a few tall trees near her back patio that provided some shade in the summer. Her neighbors on the other side were a family of four who made good use of their property by installing a massive pool—where all were welcome to jump in, and often did on hot days. Sunshine enjoyed the sound of children splashing around and playing baseball in the backyard next door.

Across the road from her property was a stay-at-home mom who ran a beauty boutique out of her house, specializing in hair and nails and of course, Sunshine was her best customer. (Sunshine was known for her long, luxurious nails and her thick, wavy hair.) When business was slow—which was often—the two friends would drive to Main Street for breakfast at the Kountry Kitchen, visit the Ramona Branch Library, or do their grocery shopping together at the supermarket.

In addition to being an active member of her community, Sunshine also served as an usher at various venues in the San Diego area. As a friend of the owner of an event staffing company, Sunshine was able to work some of the best concerts and shows that came to town and she met performers ranging from Madonna to Yo-Yo Ma.

With all she had going on, Sunshine never could find the time to write—even though she had painstakingly gathered together her complete collection of old photos (and there were thousands) as well as her notes and correspondence from over the years—boxes upon boxes, which she'd kept safe in her storage unit. Sunshine also surrounded herself with all of her favorite books, quotes, clippings, and cartoons that she'd been copying and collecting since the 1970s. Sunshine had everything she needed to write... except the discipline and desire.

"Don't you think it's weird that we're friends with the same name?" Barbara, Sunshine's neighbor and hair-stylist said while driving home from having breakfast in town.

"Not really. Nobody calls us by our real names any-way, right? I'm Sunshine, you're Bonnie, and we're total-ly different people," Sunshine pointed out.

"Did you notice that my mom called me Barbara today at the restaurant?" Bonnie asked.

"No, I didn't notice."

"She only calls me by my real name when she's mad."

"Your mom wasn't mad, she was stressed out be-cause she had to handle half the tables by herself. I've never seen the restaurant that packed before," Sunshine said.

"She's used to the Saturday crowds, I mean she's

been a waitress there for as long as I can remember. No, she seemed concerned about something else," Bonnie said as she drove through town heading back to the Country Estates area of Ramona where they both lived.

"Did you hear the firefighters at the table next to us talk about the hot, dry, windy conditions today? They seemed like they were on high alert." Sunshine mentioned, trying to change the subject.

"Those are the guys from Station 82. They come in all the time, and they're always worried about something. I wish I knew why my mom was acting so weird."

"Bonnie, it's over a hundred degrees outside and it's not even noon yet. Let's just focus on staying cool today."

"Do you have air-conditioning, Sunshine?" Bonnie asked.

"I have one in the window of my bedroom, but in the rest of the house I use fans to keep cool. I have all the drapes drawn so the house won't heat up, but it gets so dark and depressing inside that way."

"Do you want to come over and sit in my air conditioned home? I can do your nails."

"No, I'm going to work on my book today," Sunshine said.

"But it's Saturday," Bonnie stated.

"I know, but I have to get started sometime, right?"

"Okay, well, come over if it gets too hot in your house," Bonnie said as she pulled into the driveway of her stylish two-story home across the street from Sunshine's modest single-story ranch house.

"I'm off to write, wish me luck," Sunshine said as she walked across the quiet street and wondered what she was really going to do today. The truth was, she wasn't interested in working on her book. Instead of going into her house, Sunshine continued down the road to her neighbor's house. There was always something that needed to be done regarding the horses, even on a Saturday. Maybe she could cool them down, brush them out, or just keep them company. At this point, anything was more enjoyable than sitting at her desk struggling to get her thoughts on paper.

"Oh, hi Sunshine, you're here just in time to feed the horses. You wanna help? They got their exercise in early to beat the heat, so now is the perfect time for a meal, isn't that right, Charlie?" Lexi said as she put her hand on the nose of her biggest horse, a black thoroughbred Sunshine had yet to ride.

"I'm here to help with the horses any way I can."

"Good, because it's just us today. I gave everyone

the day off due to the heat. First we'll feed the horses, refill the water tanks and lastly, we can check and groom the horses. That's a full day. You sure you're up for it, Sunshine?" Lexi said as she pointed to Sunshine's choice of attire and footwear, good for going out to breakfast, bad for working with horses.

"Let me go home and change into some jeans and boots and I'll be right back," Sunshine said.

"Don't forget a hat," Lexi shouted as Sunshine hurried off to get ready, "and a scarf. It's going to get really windy later."

Sunshine put her hand up to acknowledge she'd heard Lexi's instructions as she headed home. After a quick turnaround, Sunshine spent all day working with the horses and helping out around the ranch. After all the work was done the two had dinner together then sat on Lexi's back porch and finished off a bottle of wine before switching over to coffee.

"Don't you just love how our properties run right to the edge of the mountain?" Sunshine asked.

"I know. When you face this way you would never know there are houses all around us. It's secluded, but you don't feel like you're alone, either," Lexi agreed.

"I know exactly what you mean. It's so quiet and peaceful here, but it's still a community."

One minute after Sunshine got through praising the tranquility of her new neighborhood, all hell broke loose. It started with a helicopter going overhead, which was rare since the Ramona Airport was on the other side of town. Next, the whine of sirens could be heard in the distance.

"What's going on?" Sunshine wondered aloud.

"Sunshine, look," Lexi said and pointed to a spot just over the hill as flames could be seen dancing in the distance.

Lexi stood up and tried to judge the direction of the wind. The fact they couldn't smell smoke seemed like a good sign, but with the way the wind was blowing, it was only a matter of time before they would.

"I'm sure the fire crews will get a handle on the blaze before it gets this far, but just to be on the safe side, can you help me hitch up the horse trailer to my truck?"

For the next hour the two prepared to evacuate the horses, but neither really believed it would come to that. Once they were done, they went inside to watch the news, and that's when they became convinced it was time to get out. Lexi made some calls and found a ranch on the other side of town that could and would accommodate her horses. Since Lexi would have to make four trips to move all the horses, she decided she would get going right away.

It was no easy task getting the horses into the trailer. They seemed to sense the danger and were resisting any and all instructions. Finally, they wrangled the first of the horses in and Lexi drove off as fast as she could while towing the large trailer. Sunshine agreed to stay behind and keep the remaining horses safe and calm until it was their time to be moved to safety.

The fire lit up the sky and the smoke and ashes were now making their way toward town. Lexi had dug her ski goggles out of storage and gave them to Sunshine to protect her eyes along with a handkerchief to cover her nose and mouth before she left. The horses, however, were not as lucky as smoke billowed into their stables.

Lexi came back over an hour later and brought two helpers with her so it was a lot faster loading the horses the second time, but now that other Ramona residents were evacuating, the main roads were crowded and some side streets were closed due to concerns about the path of the flames.

Sunshine was mesmerized by the fire on the mountain. It was straight out of a movie, only it was happening in her world. The fact she had worked hard all day and had not slept all night was starting to take its toll on her. Sunshine went inside to grab a cup of coffee and, since the news was still on, she could now see how serious the situation had become. Outside, police cars were driving up and down the street announcing a voluntary evacuation over the loudspeakers and at the same time encouraging residents to leave their homes behind and get out.

Sunshine peeked outside Lexi's front window and saw the neighbors helping one another hose down their homes in an attempt to ward off the flames if they came down the street. She looked over at her own house, alone in the dark, with nobody to protect it, but the animals had to come first.

By the time Lexi left with the last of the horses the flames were now roaring down the mountain toward their homes. Sunshine stood for a moment and listened to the roar of the wind and fire that sounded like a train going by. It felt like the town was under attack as sirens blared, people screamed, and firefighters rushed around trying to fight the fire as best they could. It was hard to breathe and hard to see, but she couldn't look away.

One firefighter ran through Lexi's yard and then stopped and came back. Through his face mask and protective gear he grabbed Sunshine by her shoulders and then shoved her toward the street as he shouted, "Get out of here, now!"

Sunshine ran out into the street, but she felt trapped.

There was a wall of fire directly behind Lexi's property. "Thank God we got the horses out," she thought.

She was paralyzed by fear and indecision until Bonnie ran over to her. "Sunshine, help me. I'm going door to door to make sure everyone is okay and evacuating," Bonnie yelled, pulling her up the street and away from Lexi's house.

"Shouldn't the police or fire department be doing this?" Sunshine yelled.

"Who cares, it's up to us now. Come on."

They checked on everyone they could and ended up back at Sunshine's house as the fire had intensified and the smoke thickened. "Bonnie, why is the Smith's minivan still parked in their driveway?"

"I don't know, let's go find out," Bonnie yelled as the two brave women went to check on Sunshine's next-door neighbors. "The kids, oh my God, the kids," Sunshine screamed when nobody answered the door.

"Around back, we've got to go around back," Bonnie hollered.

As soon as Bonnie and Sunshine rounded the corner of the house, they realized it was a mistake. The fire had reached Sunshine's house and her trees were ablaze. The wind was pushing the fire fast and it was heading right for them. Nothing in this world could have prepared the two for this moment, but they both reacted the same way at the same time—they jumped in the pool.

From underwater Sunshine witnessed the most amazing thing she'd ever seen as the flames passed overhead. It was terrifying and exhilarating at the same time. The surreal scene of being at the bottom of a pool with flames overhead was intense to say the least. Terrified to surface, Sunshine looked around and because she was still wearing goggles, was able to see Bonnie swimming toward the waterfall. Brilliant, she thought, that was the one place they could safely surface without being burned alive and catch their breath.

"Oh my God!" Sunshine said when she popped up.

"That was insane. We are so lucky," Bonnie blurted out between breaths.

The two friends hugged in the opening behind the waterfall and waited until it was safe to surface and see what kind of damage the fire had caused. They paused a few minutes and then swam underwater to the shallow end and with no flames above, surfaced.

What they saw was horrifying. Sunshine's home was fully engulfed in flames. There was no doubt it would burn to the ground. It wasn't until that moment that it hit her. She had brought everything with her to this house to write her book—mementos, newspaper clippings, important papers, letters and postcards, and most important of all, her pictures from years past. She didn't have much, but everything she owned was in that house. The realization of this hit her like a ton of bricks.

"Oh Sunshine, I'm so sorry. So sorry," Bonnie said.

Sunshine didn't say a word, she just dropped to her knees and cried.

DEAR DIARY. *Watching my house burn to the ground with my most prized possessions in it was devastating. It really took the wind out of my sails and it was one of the few times in my life when I truly felt like a victim. I knew I would eventually bounce back and rebuild my collection of cartoons, sayings, and books, but I also knew I would never see my precious photographs again. That hurt.*

I just kept thinking about one of my favorite quotes: "It's not what happens to you, but how you react to it that matters." I'm sure there was a reason all this happened, but I just couldn't figure out what it was.

I borrowed a car and drove down to the beach at the end of the day on Sunday and watched the sunset. It was simply amazing, in part because the fires created clouds of smoke that became beautifully backlit by the setting sun. The weather was gorgeous—like a summer's day—and the surface of the ocean was covered with ash and reflected the light in a majestic way

I'd never seen before.

I didn't know how to feel at first. I did know I wasn't going to give up, but I was going to give up a few things in my life. After a long walk on the beach, I decided I had to let go of the past and move forward. I determined that I would put off writing my book and live my life like there was no tomorrow.

Day by day not much changes, but then when you look back, everything is different. There aren't many moments in your life when everything changes all at once unless you've won millions in the lottery or been through a terrible tragedy. The Cedar Fire (the one that took my home) was the largest fire in California history, burned hundreds of homes, and took the lives of fifteen people. So, I wasn't alone, and in many respects, I was lucky.

So, instead of feeling sorry for myself, I decided I would volunteer at the evacuation site at San Diego's Qualcomm Stadium, where the Chargers play, and offer to help others who were much worse off than me. It was the best thing I could have done. I was so busy tending to the needs of others, I didn't have time to feel sorry for myself.

2010

AIN'T NO SUNSHINE
WHEN SHE'S GONE

SEVENTY-TWO YEARS OLD

"Lee, it's Sunshine," she said over the phone.

"Oh, hi, Sunshine, where are you this time? London? Paris? Rome?" I asked, since it was more of a relevant question than how she was doing, because the answer to that question was always the same—f-a-n-t-a-s-t-i-c!

"I'm in a nursing home in Hillcrest," Sunshine said matter-of-factly.

"What? What are you doing there?" I asked, not sure I heard her correctly.

"It's not only a nursing home, it's also a hospice and rehabilitation center," she said. I could sense she had something else to tell me, but she couldn't quite get it out.

"Okay, so I still don't know why *you're* there." I said hesitantly.

"I have Stage 4 lung cancer... but I'm gonna beat it," Sunshine blurted out.

"Wait, what? But, you don't even smoke. That can't be right," I stammered.

"Lee, can you come and visit me? There's something I want to talk to you about," Sunshine said, choosing to ignore my comments about her condition.

"Tell me exactly where you are and I'll be right there," I replied.

That call was like waking up to watch the Twin Towers come crashing down on September 11th—I will never forget where I was and what I was doing the day Sunshine phoned to tell me she was sick, very sick. I was driving in my car and had to pull over to talk. I stopped in a strip mall in Pacific Beach in San Diego, near where I live. After I hung up with Sunshine, I just sat there for a long time trying to let what she'd said sink in. I was simply stunned. Sunshine was the healthiest person I knew—and didn't look or act her age. In fact, I was surprised when she revealed her true age to me a week later. I had always assumed she was much younger.

I don't remember what I was supposed to be doing that day, but I do recall turning my car around and heading straight for the hospice where she was now a patient. On the way I replayed our conversation over and over again in my head. Knowing that my father died shortly after being diagnosed with Stage 4 lung cancer, I knew things did not look good for Sunshine—I also knew regardless of the diagnosis or prognosis, she would fight for her life.

On the drive downtown I wasn't sure what I would say or how I would act when I first saw her. When I walked into the facility—a place I would have otherwise avoided like the plague—I didn't know what to think. I felt sick to my stomach and close to tears, but if Sunshine wanted me there, I would be there for her and keep a positive attitude—as she would have done for me if our roles were reversed.

At the reception desk, I asked what room Sunshine was in. The receptionist was unsure there was a patient there by that name and looked at me like I was crazy. I then asked if there was a patient named Barbara Blake in residence. She checked again and said, "Oh, right, Sunshine. She's on the third floor. Take the elevator up. She's in the room right in front of you when you get off. You can't miss it."

I don't know what I expected, but to see Sunshine trapped in such a drab place devoid of any positive energy was depressing. I stood outside her room (which she shared with two other patients, separated only by a curtain) trying to gather the courage to go in. I tentatively stepped into the room and there was Sunshine sitting on the bed. She looked fearful and frail, but she managed a smile and slowly stood up. I walked over to give her a hug, but she said she had a large hole in her chest and she couldn't put any pressure on it. I understood.

Sunshine asked if I wanted to see the wound, but I knew if I did I would pass out and become a patient myself, so I declined. Sunshine showed me her "room" which was just the bed and a shelf—containing several cards, boxes of various teas, vitamins, and a large stuffed animal propped up in the corner. I think she could sense I was uncomfortable and smartly suggested we go somewhere else to talk. We walked arm-in-arm to a lounge area and sat down at a table.

We reminisced for a long time—we'd been friends for over twenty years so we had a lot of ground to cover. I could sense she didn't want me to leave. I think she felt lonely and out of place there. At one point she said, "I can't stand being around all these sick people." I didn't know what to say, so I said nothing.

"Look, it's not as bad as it sounds," Sunshine said, her hand on top of mine.

"Good, because it sounds bad," I replied.

"They say what doesn't kill you makes you stronger, and I'm not ready to die," Sunshine said, but I could tell her heart wasn't in the words.

We sat silently for a few minutes before Sunshine spoke. "The thing about facing something like this is it makes you wish you had more time to do the things you haven't done."

At this point, I didn't know half of the adventures her life had included, but I still said, "Nobody I know has lived a fuller life than you. No regrets, right?"

"I do have one regret," Sunshine said while staring deep into my eyes, "and I'm going to need your help to make it right."

"Anything, you name it," I answered, having no idea what she wanted, but willing to do whatever it was.

"I want you to write a book about me," she said, and patted the tops of both of my hands at once and then lifted them up in the air as if a huge burden had been lifted from her life.

"You want *me* to write about *you*?" I said, surprised, but not totally surprised, by the request. "What do you have in mind?"

"I leave it up to you. All I ask is that we meet once in a while so I can tell you everything you need to know to tell my story."

I sat there thinking about what that meant. Then I

LEE SILBER

stopped thinking and listened to my heart, and my heart wanted me to say "yes." The only reason I hesitated was out of fear that I wouldn't have the time to take on and tackle such an enormous endeavor.

As usual, Sunshine knew just what to say. "It has to be you."

How could I say no?

It was amazing how quickly Sunshine bounced back and was released from the facility she was staying in. Although I went to see her there one more time, we really didn't start on her book until the following week, a Wednesday—a weekday I would not book for anything else but my weekly sessions with Sunshine for months to come, by choice.

At our first meeting on the patio at Soleluna Cafe where Sunshine was a regular, and everyone knew her name, I brought along a stack of old photos of us together to review.

"Do you remember this drum circle?" I asked Sunshine, and handed her the picture.

"Oh yeah, it was at Moonlight Beach in Encinitas," Sunshine said, smiling at the shot of her banging away on a djembe, surrounded by dozens of other drummers, myself included.

"Hey, here's a picture of us with Orville Redenbacher," I said, turning the photo around so she could see us both with the popcorn icon taken at an event we put on together with several celebrities and business leaders.

"Look at this," I said while I handed Sunshine another photo of us together on my boat.

Sunshine laughed and said, "I remember your dad was down at the docks that day. I think he thought we were a couple."

"Little did he know you were both the same age," I added.

"You know, I've always wanted to tell you this, Lee. The song you wrote about your father and performed at his Celebration of Life was one of the most touching things I've ever witnessed."

I choked up a little and said, "Thank you, Sunshine."

Considering the circumstances, I wasn't sure what else to say, so Sunshine said it for me. "You don't have to write a song about me if that's what you're wondering. Someone already did that when I lived in Nashville. My husband at the time recorded "International Lady," a single about me."

That was the start of the story of her life—it wasn't in any particular order, yet we eventually covered every era of her memorable life.

The last time Sunshine and I met, she was clearly not doing well. We usually sat outside, but on this summer's day she was covered by a blanket in her wheelchair. As long as I had known her, she was always extremely fit, but now her face was gaunt and her arms were just skin and bones. For the final few weeks, she needed an oxygen tank to breathe, but she often detached it during our time together.

It was an unusual day because I had to get up early for a live interview for the local news that was being shot remotely from a bookstore in Seaport Village. I was promoting an event I was hosting there later that night. As soon as the cameras were off, I shook the host's hand and said, "I gotta go." I then rushed to the cafe around the corner to see Sunshine.

We were at the point in the process where all I needed from her was her dedication for the front of the book. Unfortunately, she was having a bad day and found it hard to focus. Deep down I knew it was time. She eventually told me the dedication she wanted to include, and I told her, "We did it. We're done." I kissed her on the cheek and then sat by her side as she nodded off. Her son said she did that a lot lately—and she could be out for a while. I understood. I knew this would be the last time I would see her.

Eventually I left and walked up the street to a park Sunshine liked to frequent because there were often children playing there. She would sit on the bench and watch them for hours. When I would walk up to meet Sunshine I would often startle her because she didn't hear me coming—she was so transfixed by the pure joy the kids were having in the playground. This day I sat there alone and watched the children play and reflected on how life goes by so fast. I now knew Sunshine's entire life story, and would tell it in 200 pages, but when she was done telling it to me, she commented that seventy years went by in the blink of an eye and reminded me not to miss it or waste it.

To my surprise, just as I was about to speak in the Upstart Crow bookstore's upstairs loft later that same day, I saw Shawn carrying his mother up the stairs in his arms. Sunshine didn't want to miss being there, despite how much pain she was in—her legs were extremely swollen and she could barely breathe—but there she was. My wife and two sons walked over to greet her and she managed a smile that lit up the room. While I was speaking to the crowd I kept looking over at Sunshine, it was hard to not cry because I knew she would be gone soon, but I smiled because she had shown me what what it meant to be a true friend. Barbara "Sunshine" Blake, my friend to the end.

DEAR DIARY (from Lee) *I stood there on the beach surrounded by Sunshine's family and friends thinking how appropriate that her sons would hold her Celebration of Life at sunset—and also, how sad. At funerals the finality of death sets in because you realize you will never see that person again, and how much you will miss them. It's hard to let go, because you don't want to.*

I found myself thinking, Sunshine would have loved this. *If I let my mind wander, I could almost believe she would come running up that beach, her long hair trailing behind her, the layers of loose-fitting clothes she loved to wear blowing in the breeze, and that familiar noise her jewelry made when she approached. Sunshine would be waving at all of us and yelling, "Hey, wait for me." Once she arrived, she would be all smiles and hug everyone and ask if they were going to be alright.*

I know it's called a "celebration of life" because those in attendance are supposed to tell stories to help you relive the best moments of the person's life before they died, but I just couldn't do it. After all the time I'd spent with Sunshine in the last year of her life, and after all she had shared with me, I just couldn't speak, and I'm not sure why. Other than her two sons, I was probably the one person who could best celebrate her life, but I didn't.

This book is my tribute to my friend. My celebration of her life. She may be gone, but now she won't be forgotten.

Lessons Learned

DEAR SUNSHINE

It pains me to write this, but there were times when out of the blue you would call to ask if I wanted to see a movie or attend a concert later that same day—or sometimes within the hour—and I would say "no." Oh how I wish I could have been more spontaneous (like you) and said "yes" more often.

There were times (many times) where you would be the first to arrive and last to leave an event I was hosting (workshops, retreats, book signings, parties, or gigs with my band) and helped set up and break down the entire thing. I'm sure I said thank you, but I regret I didn't show more appreciation for all you did.

At some of the larger events you graciously attended, I was often surrounded by people who wanted and needed my time. Sadly, sometimes I would wait until the end to talk to you because I knew you wouldn't mind. Now, I realize you were the most important person in the room at each and every event, and I should have made others wait while I took the time to be with you.

A while back, I went through my old photographs

to see which ones I wanted to scan and save. It seemed like every time I grabbed a stack of pictures there was at least one you had taken (and sent to me) or another with you in it. I saved every one and treasure them all. It pains me that I didn't save all the cards and letters you sent—many of them stuffed with quotes and cartoons—especially after you lost all of yours when your home burned to the ground.

While you were busy living your life, you didn't waste time reflecting on your past, so I never knew what an amazing life you lived until we began working on this book. Every once in a while you would let slip something about one of your great adventures, but you were too busy celebrating others' life accomplishments that you never celebrated your own. I wish I knew then what I know now about you and your life. You preferred to be behind the scenes and out of the limelight. You were the brightest star in the room, but few knew.

Many of my "friends" would make excuses about why they didn't buy my latest book or attend the related release party. Not only did you make it to every single event, you would also purchase a dozen books to give as gifts. I know I appreciated the support and the sales, but now I wish I had just given you the books—as many as you wanted—for your unwavering support over the years.

Since the first time I met you at a publishing forum I was hosting at a Barnes and Noble you always said you wanted to write a book—but never did. Writing a book for and about you was the most joyous and satisfying experience I've ever had as an author. I only wish you were here to read it.

From the moment you told me you were dying (although you never put it quite that way), I decided this was my opportunity to be there for you. I cherished our Wednesdays together as we reminisced over long lunches at Soleluna Cafe. I vowed to never miss a meeting with you, to put you first and let you shine for once, to be there for you no matter what, and to try to repay you by doing something for you that you weren't able to do for yourself.

I was touched and honored you chose me to tell your story—and more than that, I was so lucky you chose me to be your friend. There was a warm light that followed you around and enveloped anyone near you. I felt it every time we met, which is why I loved our time together. Your words motivated me, your life lessons educated me, and the way you dealt with life (and death) inspired me. Now that you are gone, I miss you and there's a hole in my heart that to this day can't be filled.

Love,

LIFE LESSONS

If you skipped to this section without reading the book, congratulations. That's what Sunshine would have done, too. If you did read the book you can probably guess what Sunshine's main message was. Either way, I included the seven life lessons I am sure she would want to tell you if she could.

LIFE LESSON 1 / NO EXCUSES

Don't use your past as an excuse for not living a full and fruitful life today. No matter how bad you had it growing up, Sunshine suffered worse, but she chose to not let her past determine her future. "Where you come from isn't as important as where you are going," she would often say. Don't use your early life as an excuse for your future problems and failures as an adult. Whining about how you were mistreated or wronged makes you look like a victim, and the last thing Sunshine wanted to be seen as was helpless. Instead, she used what burned her up as fuel for the fire that motivated her to take charge of her life and make things happen despite her terrible childhood. Don't blame others, instead learn to make better choices.

LIFE LESSON 2 / OPPORTUNITIES ARE EVERYWHERE

The universe provides you with everything you need to succeed and find happiness. Everywhere you turn opportunities are presented to you. These opportunities are sent to you as a gift. What you do with these chances determines what your life becomes. Pay attention to what the universe is trying to tell you to do—and then do it, knowing it was a personal invitation to change and improve your life. Sunshine believed in abundance. She felt that around every corner (even after a "failure") the next big thing was waiting for her and she would keep a watchful eye out for any sign as to what it might be. "If you believe it will work out, you'll see opportunities. If you believe it won't, you will see obstacles," said Wayne Dyer, who like Sunshine, shuffled between foster families.

LIFE LESSON 3 / NO REGRETS

Live life to the fullest—travel, meet people, fall in love, love what you do, but don't wait until it's too late. "Happiness is not something you postpone for the future—it is something you design for the present," said Jim Rohn, Sunshine's favorite person to quote. To Sunshine, we are the sum total of our experiences and doing things is better than owning things. She hated the phrase, "Time is money," and would often remind the person who said it that time is far more valuable than money, so spend it wisely. Time equals our life, which means we use our time to earn the money to buy the material things we own. Since we trade our time for money (working, commuting, shopping) we should be careful about what we spend it on. Some people sit on the couch (or in an office or a car stuck in traffic) watching life pass them by looking out of a window or watching television. Sunshine would say to them, "Get out there and live your life and see things for yourself. Live like there is no tomorrow—because there may not be one."

LIFE LESSON 4 / SAY YES

Just say "yes" was Sunshine's philosophy because she wasn't afraid of failing, hearing "no," or looking silly. She wouldn't let what she couldn't do interfere with what she could do. Sunshine believed fear holds us back from our true potential, so she would try doing something every day that scared her so she was comfortable with both fear and failure—and it worked. Things always work out and worrying about outcomes creates fear. When we just act and react we are much better at what we do. One of

Sunshine's favorite quotes was from hockey great Wayne Gretsky. "You miss 100 percent of the shots you never take." So she took chances because she believed it was better to try and fail than not to try at all. What Sunshine was afraid of was missing out on an opportunity.

LIFE LESSON 5 / MAKE MEMORIES

To Sunshine, the best gift she could give or get was a photograph. Her favorite thing to do was capture and celebrate the magic moments in her life (and yours) and share them. Since she saw so much change in her life, she was aware that some things would happen only once, and she wanted to remember and revisit that moment in time long after it passed. C. S. Lewis said, "It's funny how day by day, nothing changes. But when you look back, everything is different." Stopping to take a picture to slow down time allowed her to appreciate and celebrate something others may have missed. Today we have no excuse to not stop time with a picture (or video) since we have the perfect tool (a smart phone) in our pocket or purse to do so. Before social media, Sunshine sent pictures (through the mail) as a way to stay connected with people. I know I was the recipient of hundreds of photos over the years. These pictures make me smile at the memory and keep Sunshine in the forefront of my thoughts.

LIFE LESSON 6 / DON'T WORRY, BE HAPPY

Everything happens for a reason. Sometimes your seemingly bad luck turns out to be good luck in the end. Whatever happens to you may help you later on and be the best thing that could have happened in hindsight. If we could all take a page from Sunshine's book and just let go and let things happen and trust that no matter what, everything will work out, we'd have a lot less stress. Sure, she was always upbeat and optimistic, but as she would say, the alternative is to focus on the negative and you get what you focus on. To her, attitude was everything—and a positive attitude is better than a negative one. If we head for the light, we will be fine because where we end up is where we were supposed to be all along. Sunshine believed there are no accidents and everything—good and bad—happens for a reason.

LIFE LESSON 7 / LIVE YOUR TRUTH

Don't be so concerned with what others think of you. Instead, you should be more concerned with what you think of yourself. In other words, live your truth. Do what feels right (as long as it doesn't hurt you or others). Don't worry what others will say or think. You have to live your life the way you want. You are in charge of your life. What makes you happy and brings you joy? Pursue that, because as Marsha Sinetar said, "Do what you love and the money will follow." Sunshine's theory was it is better to give than to get and always asked, "What can I give?" If you selflessly give others what they want you will always get what you need. Let people know how much you care about them and they will be there when you need them most.

For more of Sunshine's Life Lessons, go to www.leesilber.com.

DISCUSSION

I am sure there are many questions you have after reading this book. Here are a few I anticipated, along with my answers. You can always reach out to me at the address below and I can answer any other questions you may have.

IS SUNSHINE A REAL PERSON?

Yes. Sunshine was born on January 11, 1938, in Easton, Pennsylvania. Her real name was Barbara Ann Begies, but everyone called her Sunshine. In fact, I had to ask her son for her actual last name. She went by Sunshine Blake for as long as I knew her, but I also knew it wasn't her original surname.

HOW MUCH OF THE BOOK IS BASED ON REAL EVENTS?

This book proves that truth is stranger than fiction. Nearly everything that happens in the book happened in real life. The people, places, and things she told me about found their way into the story. The book started out as a biography but became factual fiction, because for a time even I doubted some of the details of Sunshine's story.

While I listened intently to Sunshine tell me about her fantastical life, I diligently took notes about everything she said—while I wondered to myself if it really happened or if she had dreamed all of it up. When I began researching the things she told me about, I quickly realized what she had shared with me (in great detail) checked out. It's hard to believe all of these things happened to one woman—but Sunshine was no ordinary woman, she was extraordinary. In fact, I didn't include many of the things she did—run with bulls in Pamplona and walk the Great Wall of China to name just two—because it would have made the book too long.

There were two things she mentioned to me about her life that I couldn't verify—one of which was meeting Albert Einstein, another was about befriending famous artist Edith Halpert—so I left them out of the novel. I wouldn't be surprised if they were both true, but I was unable to find out for sure. (Sunshine did live just one town over from Princeton during the same years Einstein was there.)

Otherwise, I took the facts as told to me by Sunshine and then used a lot of literary license to make them come to life. I think it's important for readers to remember this is a novel, so I did make up some situations and several conversations, but I was able to follow the timeline of her life and use her words as told to me, throughout the book.

HOW OFTEN DID YOU MEET WITH SUNSHINE IN HER FINAL YEAR?

Just after she was diagnosed with Stage 4 lung cancer, Sunshine and I met twice a month (usually on Wednesdays) at some of her favorite places around town. She and I would sit and talk—actually, she talked and I listened. I could tell she enjoyed sharing her adventures with me and made it a point to also make sure I was aware of the lessons she learned along the way.

As her condition worsened—in the final few months of her life, she required an oxygen tank to breathe—we met more often, but only at Soleluna Cafe, her favorite eatery in San Diego. (The cafe was close to where she lived and offers excellent cuisine and coffee.)

Her son Shawn moved down from Los Angeles to help his mom get around and he would sometimes sit in on our sessions. He was very helpful in filling in some of the gaps in his mom's memory—he had to remind her she was married six times, not just the four times she could recall.

In our last official meeting (I would see Sunshine one last time before she passed away), I asked her to tell me who she wanted to dedicate the book to. It was the last thing I needed from her before I could begin writing.

WHAT TOOK YOU SO LONG TO FINISH THE BOOK?

It's a huge responsibility to get it right when someone entrusts you to tell their life story. It's also a daunting task to condense over seventy years of a life—and one filled with so many ups and downs and twists and turns—into a 200-plus-page book.

The turning point came when I had the idea to turn the biography into a novel. Once that happened, I couldn't wait to write. In fact, there were days I would write for hours on end and get so absorbed in the story I would forget to eat lunch or drink enough water.

One factor that did slow up the process was my desire to make sure that I was not only true to Sunshine's life story, but that I also was true to the back story. It would sometimes take a week just to research some of the places she lived, the people she met (many of them famous), and the things she did. I wanted to make sure that if she said she drove a certain type of van, that the make and model was indeed available in the style and color she said it was. In the process, I became a semi-expert on several subjects I didn't know a thing about before I began writing this book.

WHERE WERE HER CHILDREN WHEN SHE WAS TRAVELING ABROAD?

Ah, I knew this question was coming. In the book it appears as if sometimes the kids are with her and sometimes they are not, which is the truth. Sunshine did take the boys on some of her adventures, and other times they were either in boarding school or staying with family and friends. Sunshine always made sure they were both safe and well cared for when she wasn't there to care for them herself.

WHAT DO YOU THINK SUNSHINE WOULD THINK OF HER BOOK?

I asked myself this very same question a lot, and it shaped the way I wrote this book. I knew Sunshine extremely well so I could write the way she spoke with ease, but I also knew that she wouldn't be around to edit or change what I wrote, so I left out a few things that I thought might embarrass her if she were here.

ARE THERE ANY QUESTIONS YOU WISH YOU COULD ASK HER NOW?

There are so many things I wish I could have asked her about when I was writing the book. Certain things she told me about when we met didn't seem to warrant further explanation at the time, but now I know I could have used a lot more details about a great many of the things she just glossed over in the retelling of her life.

HOW DO WE GET HOLD OF YOU TO ASK OTHER QUESTIONS?

You can reach me through my website: www.leesilber.com. Don't hesitate to reach out because as you have probably guessed, any friend of Sunshine's is a friend of mine.

If you have other questions or would like to have Lee come to your book club or have him speak to your organization or association, contact him at leesilber@leesilber.com.

WISE WORDS

Sunshine was always sending cartoons, newspaper clippings, and quotes through the mail. (Oh, how she would have loved social media.) During one of our long lunches I asked Sunshine to give me her five favorite quotations, and the following are the five she recited verbatim and without hesitation, plus one more... which was so Sunshine.

"Don't wish it were easier; wish you were better."

—JIM ROHN

"It's not what happens to you that matters, but how you react to it that matters."

—EPICTETUS

"If you have time to whine and complain about something, then you have the time to do something about it."

—ANTHONY J. D'ANGELO

"Life is trying things to see if they work."

—RAY BRADBURY

"Don't let what you can't do interfere with what you can do."

—JOHN WOODEN

"We make a living by what we get; we make a life by what we give."

—WINSTON CHURCHILL

For more of Sunshine's favorite quotations, go to www.leesilber.com.

ABOUT THE AUTHOR

Lee Silber is the award-winning author of 21 books, including 18 works of non-fiction, two novels, and one book of short stories. This book is a unique combination of both fact and fiction, and wouldn't have been possible without Silber's extensive experience writing in both genres. Everything up to this point in Lee's life led him to write this book—and write it for his friend, Sunshine.

In addition to sharing Sunshine's story in print, Silber brings her lessons to life in his presentations by teaching and sharing innovative and insightful ways to get the most from your time and talent. Lee is a highly sought-after public speaker working with organizations both big and small to make a difference by encouraging audiences to think, laugh, and learn.

Lee lives in Mission Beach, California with his wife and two sons.

LEESILBER@LEESILBER.COM

Made in the USA
Las Vegas, NV
03 July 2024